Little Lame Prince

No one in the land was happier with the birth of the prince than his parents, the King and Queen. And no one was more disappointed than his uncle—the Crown Prince—who would have been the heir to the throne had the little boy not been born.

With the death of the King and Queen, the prince is left in the care of his jealous uncle, who secretly sends the child away to a distant and desolate tower. There, he would have remained a helpless prisoner...had it not been for his fairy godmother! It is she who gives the lonely child a magic traveling cloak, which enables him to go where his little lame legs cannot take him. And it is with her help that the prince discovers his true identity and reclaims his rightful throne.

The Little Lame Prince

Dinah Maria Mulock Craik

A WATERMILL CLASSIC

Contents of this edition copyright © 1983 by Watermill Press,
Mahwah, New Jersey.

Printed in the United States of America.

ISBN 0-89375-710-1

Chapter 1

Yes, he was the most beautiful Prince that ever was born.

Of course, being a prince, people said this; but it was true besides. When he looked at the candle, his eyes had an expression of earnest inquiry quite startling in a newborn baby. His nose—there was not much of it certainly, but what there was seemed an aquiline shape. His complexion was a charming, healthy purple. He was round and fat, straight-limbed and long—in fact, a splendid baby. Everybody was exceedingly proud of him, especially his father and mother, the King and Queen of Nomansland, who had waited for him during their happy reign of ten years—now made happier than ever, to themselves and their subjects, by the appearance of a son and heir.

The only person who was not quite happy was the King's brother, the heir presumptive, who would have been king one day had the baby not been born. But as his Majesty was very kind to him, and even rather sorry for him—insomuch that at the Queen's request he gave him a dukedom almost as big as a county—the Crown Prince, as he was called, tried to seem pleased also; and let us hope he succeeded.

The Prince's christening was to be a grand affair. According to the custom of the country, there were chosen for him four-and-twenty godfathers and godmothers, who each had to give him a name, and promise to do their utmost for him. When he came of age, he himself had to choose the name—and the godfather or godmother—that he liked best, for the rest of his days.

Meantime all was rejoicing. Subscriptions were made among the rich to give pleasure to the poor; dinners in town halls for the working-men; tea parties in the streets for their wives; and milk-and-bun feasts for the children in the schoolrooms. For Nomansland, though I cannot point it out on any map or read of it in any history, was, I believe, much like our own or many another country.

As for the palace—which was no different from other palaces—it was clean "turned out of the windows," as people say, with the preparations going on. The only quiet place in it was the room which, though the Prince was six weeks old, his mother the Queen had never quitted. Nobody said she was ill, however—it would have been so inconvenient. And as she said nothing about it herself, but lay pale and placid, giving no trouble to anybody, nobody thought much about her. All the world was absorbed in admiring the baby.

The christening day came at last, and it was as lovely as the Prince himself. All the people in the palace were lovely too—or thought themselves so—in the elegant new clothes which the Queen, who thought of everybody, had taken care to give them, from the ladies-in-waiting down to the poor little kitchen maid, who looked at herself in her pink cotton gown, and thought, doubtless, that there never was such a pretty girl as she.

By six in the morning all the royal household had dressed itself in its very best. And then the little Prince was dressed in his best—his magnificent christening robe; which proceeding his Royal Highness did not like at all, but kicked and screamed like any common baby. When he had calmed down a little, they carried him to be looked at by the Queen his mother, who, though her royal robes had been brought and laid upon the bed, was, as everybody well knew, quite unable to rise and put them on.

She admired her baby very much; kissed and blessed him, and lay looking at him, as she did for hours sometimes, when he was placed beside her fast asleep. Then she gave him up with a gentle smile, and, saying she hoped he would be very good, that it would be a very nice christening, and all the guests would enjoy themselves, turning peacefully over on her bed, saying nothing more to anybody. She was a very uncomplaining person, the Queen—and her name was Dolorez.

Everything went on exactly as if she had been present. All, even the King himself, had grown used to her absence; for she was not strong, and for years had not joined in any gaieties. She always did her royal duties, but as to pleasures, they could go on quite well without her, or it seemed so. The company arrived: great and notable persons in this and neighboring countries; also the four-and-twenty godfathers and godmothers, who had been chosen with care, as the people who would be most useful to his Royal Highness should he ever want friends, which did not seem likely. What such want could possibly happen to the heir of the powerful monarch of Nomansland?

They came, walking two and two, with their coronets on their heads—being dukes and duchesses, princes and princesses, or the like. They all kissed the child and pronounced the name each had given him. Then the four-and-twenty names were shouted out with great energy by six heralds, one after the other, and afterward written down, to be preserved in the state records, in readiness for the next time they were wanted, which would be either on his Royal Highness's coronation or his funeral.

Soon the ceremony was over, and everybody satisfied; except, perhaps, the little Prince himself, who moaned faintly under his christening robes, which nearly smothered him.

In truth, though very few knew, the Prince in coming to the chapel had met with a slight disaster. His nurse—not his ordinary one, but the state nursemaid—an elegant and fashionable young lady of rank whose duty it was to carry him to and from the chapel, had been so occupied in arranging her train with one hand, while she held the baby with the other, that she stumbled and let him fall, just at the foot of the marble staircase.

To be sure, she contrived to pick him up again the next minute; and the accident was so slight it seemed hardly worth speaking of. Consequently nobody did speak of it. The baby had turned deadly pale, but did not cry, so no person a step or two behind could discover anything wrong. Afterward, even if he had moaned, the silver trumpets were loud enough to drown his noise. It would have been a pity to let anything trouble such a day of felicity.

So, after a minute's pause, the procession had moved on. Such a procession! Heralds in blue and silver; pages in crimson and gold; and a troop of little girls in dazzling white, carrying baskets of flowers, which they strewed all the way before the nurse and child. Finally the four-and-twenty godfathers and godmothers, as proud as possible, and so splendid to look at that they would have, quite extinguished their small godson—merely a heap of lace and muslin with a baby face inside—had it not been for a canopy of white satin and ostrich feather which was held over him wherever he was carried.

Thus, with the sun shining on them through the painted windows, they stood; the King and his train on one side, the Prince and his attendants on the other, as pretty a sight as ever was seen out of fairyland.

"It's just like a fairyland," whispered the eldest little girl to the next eldest, as she shook the last rose out of her basket; "and I think the only thing the Prince wants now is a fairy god-mother."

"Does he?" said a shrill but soft and not unpleasant voice behind; and there was seen among the group of children somebody—not a child, yet not bigger than a child—somebody whom nobody had seen before, and who certainly had not been invited, for she had no christening clothes on.

She was a little woman dressed all in gray: gray gown; gray hooded cloak, of a material excessively fine, and a tint that seemed perpetually changing, like the gray of an evening sky. Her hair was gray, and her eyes also—even her complexion had a soft gray shadow over it. But there was nothing unpleas-antly old about her, and her smile was as sweet and childlike as the Prince's own, which stole over his pale little face the instant she came near enough to touch him.

"Take care! Don't let the baby fall again."

The grand young lady nurse started, flushing angrily.

"Who spoke to me? How did anybody know? —I mean, what business has anybody—" Then, frightened, but still speaking in a much sharper tone than I hope young ladies of rank are in the habit of speaking—"Old woman, you will be kind enough not to say 'the baby,' but 'the Prince.' Keep away; his Royal Highness is just going to sleep."

"Nevertheless I must kiss him. I am his god-mother."

"You!" cried the elegant lady nurse.

"You!!!" repeated all the gentlemen-and ladies-in-waiting.

"You!" echoed the heralds and pages—and they began to blow the silver trumpets in order to stop all further conversation.

The Prince's procession formed itself for returning—the King and his train having already moved off toward the palace—but on the topmost step of the marble stairs stood, right in front of all, the little old woman clothed in gray.

She stretched herself on tiptoe by the help of her stick, and gave the little Prince three kisses.

"This is intolerable!" cried the young lady nurse, wiping the kisses off rapidly with her lace handkerchief. "Such an insult to his Royal Highness! Take yourself out of the way, old woman, or the King shall be informed immediately."

"The King knows nothing of me, more's the pity," replied the old woman, with an indifferent air, as if she thought the loss was more on his Majesty's side than hers. "My friend in the palace is the King's wife."

"Kings have not wives, but queens," said the lady nurse, with a contemptuous air.

"You are right," replied the old woman. "Nevertheless, I know her Majesty well, and I love her and her child. And—since you dropped him on the marble stairs [this she said in a mysterious whisper, which made the young lady tremble in spite of her anger]—I choose to take him for my own, and be his godmother, ready to help him whenever he wants me."

"You help him!" cried all the group, breaking into shouts of laughter, to which the little old woman paid not the slightest attention. Her soft gray eyes were fixed on the Prince, who seemed to answer to the look, smiling again and again in the causeless, aimless fashion that babies do smile.

"His Majesty must hear of this," said a gentleman-in-waiting.

"His Majesty will hear quite enough news in a minute or two," said the old woman sadly. And again stretching up to the little Prince, she kissed him on the forehead solemnly.

"Be called by a new name which nobody had ever thought of. Be Prince Dolor, in memory or your mother Dolorez."

"In memory of!" Everybody started at the ominous phrase, and also at a most terrible breach of etiquette which the old woman had committed. In Nomansland, neither the King nor the Queen was supposed to have any Christian name at all. They dropped it on their coronation day, and it never was mentioned again till it was engraved on their coffins when they died.

"Old woman, you are exceedingly ill-bred," cried the eldest lady-in-waiting, much horrified. "How you could know the fact passes my comprehension. But even if you did know it, how dared you presume to hint that her most gracious Majesty is called Dolorez?"

"*Was* called Dolorez," said the old woman, with a tender solemnity.

The first gentleman, called the goldstick-in-waiting, raised it to strike her, and all the rest stretched out their hands to seize her; but the gray mantle melted from between their fingers like air. And, before anybody had time to do anything more, there came a heavy, muffled, startling sound.

The great bell of the palace—the bell which was heard only on the death of someone of the royal family, and for as many times as he or she was years old—began to toll. They listened, mute and horror-stricken. Someone counted: One—two—three—four—up to nine-and-twenty—just the Queen's age.

It was, indeed, the Queen. Her Majesty was dead! In the midst of the festivities she had slipped away out of her new happiness and her old sufferings, not few nor small. Sending away all her women to see the grand sight—at least they said afterward, in excuse, that she had done so, and it was very like her to do it—she had turned with her face to the window, whence one could just see the tops of the distant mountains—the Beautiful Mountains, as they were called—where she was born. So gazing, she had quietly passed away.

When the little Prince was carried back to his mother's room, there was no mother to kiss him. And, though he did not know it, there would be for him no mother's kiss anymore.

As for his godmother—the little old woman in

9

gray who called herself so—whether she melted into air, like her gown when they touched it, or whether she flew out the chapel window, or slipped through the doorway among the bewildered crowd, nobody knew—nobody ever thought about her.

Only the nurse, the ordinary homely one, coming out of the Prince's nursery in the middle of the night in search of a cordial to quiet his continual moans, saw, sitting in the doorway, something which she would have thought a mere shadow had she not seen shining out of it two eyes, gray and soft and sweet. She put her hands before her own, screaming loudly. When she took them away the old woman was gone.

Chapter 2

Everybody was very kind to the poor little Prince. I think people generally are kind to motherless children, whether princes or peasants. He had a magnificent nursery and a regular suite of attendants, and was treated with the greatest respect and state. Nobody was allowed to talk to him in silly baby language, or dandle him, or above all to kiss him, though perhaps so people did it surreptitiously, for he was such a sweet baby that it was difficult to help it.

It could not be said that the Prince missed his mother—children of his age cannot do that; but somehow after she died everything seemed to go wrong with him. From a beautiful baby he became sickly and pale, seeming to have almost ceased growing, especially in his legs, which had been so fat and strong.

But after the day of his christening they

withered and shrank. He no longer kicked them out in either passion or play, and when, as he got to be nearly a year old, his nurse tried to make him stand upon them, he only tumbled down.

This happened so many times that at last people began to talk about it. A prince, and not able to stand on his own legs! What a dreadful thing! What a misfortune for the country!

Rather a misfortune to him also, poor little boy! but nobody seemed to think of that. And when, after a while, his health revived, and the old bright look came back to his sweet little face, and his body grew larger and stronger, though still his legs remained the same, people continued to speak of him in whispers, and with grave shakes of the head. Everybody knew, though nobody said it, that something, it was impossible to guess what, was not quite right with the poor little Prince.

Of course, nobody hinted this to the King his father. It does not do to tell great people anything unpleasant. And besides, his Majesty took very little notice of his son, or of his other affairs, beyond the necessary duties of his kingdom.

People had said he would not miss the Queen at all, she having been so long an invalid, but he did. After her death he never was quite the same. He established himself in her empty rooms, the only rooms in the palace whence one could see the Beautiful Mountains, and was often observed looking at them as if he thought she had flown away thither, and that his longing could bring her back again. And by a curious coincidence, which nobody dared inquire into, he desired that the Prince might be called, not by any of the four-and-twenty grand names given him by his godfathers and godmothers, but by the identical name mentioned by the little old woman in gray—Dolor, after his mother Dolorez.

Once a week, according to established state custom, the Prince, dressed in his very best, was brought to the King his father for half an hour, but his Majesty was generally too ill and too melancholy to pay much heed to the child.

Only once, when he and the Crown Prince, who was exceedingly attentive to his royal brother, were sitting together, with Prince Dolor playing in a corner of the room, dragging himself about with his arms rather than his legs, and sometimes trying feebly to crawl from one chair to another, it seemed to strike the father that all was not right with his son.

"How old is his Royal Highness?" said he suddenly to the nurse.

"Two years, three months, and five days, please your Majesty."

"It does not please me," said the King, with a sigh. "He ought to be far more forward than he is now—ought he not, brother? You, who have so many children, must know. Is there not something wrong about him?"

"Oh, no," said the Crown Prince, exchanging meaning looks with the nurse, who did not understand at all, but stood frightened and trembling with the tears in her eyes.

"Nothing to make your Majesty at all uneasy. No doubt his Royal Highness will outgrow it in time."

"Outgrow—what?"

"A slight delicacy—ahem!—in the spine; something inherited, perhaps, from his mother."

"Ah, she was always delicate; but she was the sweetest woman that ever lived. Come here, my little son."

And as the Prince turned round upon his father a small, sweet, grave face—so like his mother's—his Majesty the King smiled and held out his arms. But when the boy came to him, not running like a boy, but wriggling awkwardly along the floor, the royal countenance clouded over.

"I ought to have been told of this. It is terrible—terrible! And for a prince too. Send for all the doctors in my kingdom immediately."

They came, and each gave a different opinion and ordered a different mode of treatment. The only thing they agreed in was what had been pretty well known before, that the Prince must have been hurt when he was an infant—let fall, perhaps, so as to injure his spine and lower limbs. Did nobody remember?

No, nobody. Indignantly, all the nurses denied that any such accident had happened, was possible to have happened, until the faithful country nurse recollected that it really had happened on the day of the christening. For which unluckily good memory all the others scolded her so severely that she had no peace of her life, and soon after, by the influence of the young lady nurse who had carried the baby that fatal day, and who was a sort of connection of the Crown Prince—being his wife's second cousin once removed—the poor woman was pensioned off and sent to the Beautiful Mountains from whence she came, with orders to remain there for the rest of her days.

But of all this the King knew nothing, for, indeed, after the first shock of finding out that his son could not walk, and seemed never likely to walk, he interfered very little concerning him. The whole thing was too painful, and his Majesty never liked painful things. Sometimes he inquired after Prince Dolor, and they told him his Royal Highness was going on as well as could be expected, which really was the case. For, after worrying the poor child and perplexing themselves with one remedy after another, the Crown Prince, not wishing to offend any of the differing doctors, had proposed leaving him to Nature; and Nature, the safest doctor of all, had come to his help and done her best.

He could not walk, it is true. His limbs were mere useless appendages to his body; but the body itself was strong and sound. And his face was the same as ever—just his mother's face, one of the sweetest in the world.

Even the King, indifferent as he was, sometimes looked at the little fellow with sad tenderness, noticing how cleverly he learned to crawl and swing himself about by his arms, so that in his own awkward way he was as active in motion as most children of his age.

"Poor little man! he does his best, and he is not unhappy—not half so unhappy as I, brother," addressing the Crown Prince, who was more constant than ever in his attendance upon the sick monarch. "If anything should befall me, I have appointed you Regent. In case of my death, you will take care of my poor little boy?"

"Certainly, certainly; but do not let us imagine any such misfortune. I assure your Majesty—everybody will assure you—that it is not in the least likely."

He knew, however, and everybody knew, that it was likely, and soon after it actually did happen. The King died as suddenly and quietly as the Queen had done—indeed, in her room and bed; and Prince Dolor was left without either father or mother—as sad a thing as could happen, even to a prince.

He was more than that now, though. He was a king. In Nomansland, as in other countries, the people were struck with grief one day and revived the next. "The King is dead—long live the King!" was the cry that rang through the nation, and almost before his late Majesty had been laid beside the Queen in their splendid mausoleum, crowds came thronging from all parts to the royal palace, eager to see the new monarch.

They did see him—the Prince Regent took care they should—sitting on the floor of the council chamber, sucking his thumb! And when one of the gentlemen-in-waiting lifted him up and carried him—fancy carrying a king!—to the chair of state, and put the crown on his head, he shook it off again, it was so heavy and uncomfortable. Sliding down to the foot of the throne he began playing with the golden lions that supported it, stroking their paws and putting his tiny fingers into their eyes, and laughing—laughing as if he had at last found something to amuse him.

"There's a fine king for you!" said the first lord-in-waiting, a friend of the Prince Regent's (the Crown Prince that used to be, who, in the deepest mourning, stood silently beside the throne of his young nephew; he was a handsome man, very grand· and clever-looking). "What a king! who can never stand to receive his subjects, never walk in processions, who to the last day of his life will have to be carried about like a baby. Very unfortunate!"

"Exceedingly unfortunate," repeated the second lord. "It is always bad for a nation when its king is a child; but such a child—a permanent cripple, if not worse."

"Let us hope not worse," said the first lord in a very hopeless tone, and looking toward the Regent, who stood erect and pretended to hear nothing. "I have heard that these children with very large heads, and great broad foreheads and staring eyes, are—well, well, let us hope for the best and be prepared for the worst. In the meantime—"

"I swear," said the Crown Prince, coming forward and kissing the hilt of his sword—"I swear to perform my duties as Regent, to take all care of his Royal Highness—his Majesty, I mean,'' with a grand bow to the little child, who laughed innocently back again. ''And I will do my best to govern the country. Still, if the country has the slightest objection—''

But the Crown Prince being generalissimo, having the whole army at his beck and call, so that he could have begun a civil war in no time, the country had, of course, not the slightest objection.

So the King and Queen slept in their tomb in peace, and Prince Dolor reigned over the land— that is, his uncle did; and everybody said what a fortunate thing it was for the poor little Prince to have such a clever uncle to take care of him.

All things went on as usual. Indeed, after the Regent had brought his wife and her seven sons, and established them in the palace, they went on rather better than usual. For they gave such splendid entertainments and made the capital so lively that trade revived, and the country was said to be more flourishing than it had been for a century.

Whenever the Regent and his sons appeared, they were received with shouts: ''Long live the Crown Prince!'' ''Long live the royal family!'' And, in truth, they were very fine children, the whole seven of them, and made a great show when they road out together on seven beautiful horses, one height above another, down to the youngest, on his tiny black pony, no bigger than a large dog.

As for the other child, his Royal Highness Prince Dolor—for somehow people soon ceased to call him his Majesty, which seemed such a ridiculous title for a poor little fellow, a helpless cripple

—with only head and trunk, and no legs to speak of—he was seen very seldom by anybody.

Sometimes people daring enough to peer over the high walls of the palace garden noticed there, carried in a footman's arms, or drawn in a chair, or left to play on the grass, often with nobody to mind him, a pretty little boy, with a bright, intelligent face and large, melancholy eyes—no, not exactly melancholy, for they were his mother's, and she was by no means sad-minded, but thoughtful and dreamy. They rather perplexed people, those childish eyes; they were so exceedingly innocent and yet so penetrating. If anybody did a wrong thing —told a lie, for instance—they would turn round with such a grave, silent surprise—the child never talked much—that every naughty person in the palace was rather afraid of Prince Dolor.

He could not help it, and perhaps he did not even know it, being no better a child than many other children, but there was something about him which made bad people sorry, and grumbling people ashamed of themselves, and ill-natured people gentle and kind.

I suppose because they were touched to see a poor little fellow who did not in the least know what had befallen him or what lay before him, living his baby life as happily as the day is long. Thus, whether or not he was good himself, the sight of him and his affliction made other people good, and, above all, made everybody love him—so much so that his uncle the Regent began to feel a little uncomfortable.

Now, I have nothing to say against uncles in general. They are usually very excellent people, and very convenient to little boys and girls. Even the "cruel uncle" of the *Babes in the Wood* I believe to be quite an exceptional character. And this "cruel uncle" of whom I am telling was, I hope, an exception, too.

He did not mean to be cruel. If anybody had called him so, he would have resented it extremely. He would have said that what he did was done entirely for the good of the country. But he was a man who had always been accustomed to consider himself first and foremost, believing that whatever he wanted was sure to be right, and therefore he ought to have it. So he tried to get it, and got it too, as people like him very often do. Whether they enjoy it when they have it is another question.

Therefore he went one day to the council chamber, determined on making a speech, and informing the ministers and the country at large that the young King was in failing health, and that it would be advisable to send him for a time to the Beautiful Mountains. Whether he really meant to do this, or whether it occurred to him afterward that there would be an easier way of attaining his great desire, the crown of Nomansland, is a point which I cannot decide.

But soon after, when he had obtained an order in council to send the King away—which was done in great state, with a guard of honor composed of two whole regiments of soldiers—the nation learned, without much surprise, that the poor little Prince—nobody ever called him

King now—had gone on a much longer journey than to the Beautiful Mountains.

He had fallen ill on the road and died within a few hours; at least so declared the physician in attendance and the nurse who had been sent to take care of him. They brought his coffin back in great state, and buried it in the mausoleum with his parents.

So Prince Dolor was seen no more. The country went into deep mourning for him, and then forgot him, and his uncle reigned in his stead. That illustrious personage accepted his crown with great decorum, and wore it with great dignity to the last. But whether he enjoyed it or not there is no evidence to show.

Chapter 3

And what of the little lame Prince, whom everybody seemed so easily to have forgotten?

Not everybody. There were a few kind souls, mothers of families, who had heard his sad story, and some servants about the palace, who had been familiar with his sweet ways—these many a time sighed and said, "Poor Prince Dolor!" Or, looking at the Beautiful Mountains, which were visible all over Nomansland, though few people ever visited them, "Well, perhaps his Royal Highness is better where he is than even there."

They did not know—indeed, hardly anybody did know—that beyond the mountains, between them and the sea, lay a tract of country, barren, level, bare, except for short, stunted grass, and here and there a patch of tiny flowers. Not a bush—not a tree—not a resting place for bird or beast was in that dreary plain. In summer the sunshine fell upon it hour after hour with blinding glare. In winter the winds and rains swept over it unhindered, and the snow came down steadily, noiselessly, covering it from end to end in one great white sheet, which lay for days and weeks unmarked by a single footprint.

Not a pleasant place to live in—and nobody did live there, apparently. The only sign that human creatures had ever been near the spot was one large round tower which rose up in the center of the plain, and might be seen from every part of it—if there had been anybody to see, which there never was. Rose right up out of the ground, as if it had grown of itself, like a mushroom. But it was not at all mushroomlike; on the contrary, it was very solidly built. In form it resembled the Irish round towers, which have puzzled people for so long, nobody being able to find out when, or by whom, or for what purpose they were made; seemingly for no use at all, like this tower. It was circular, of very firm brickwork, with neither doors nor windows, until near the top, when you could perceive some slits in the wall through which one might possibly creep in or look out. Its height was nearly a hundred feet, and it had a battlemented parapet showing sharp against the sky.

As the plain was quite desolate—almost like a desert, only without sand, and led to nowhere except the still more desolate seacoast—nobody ever crossed it. Whatever mystery there was about the tower, it and the sky and the plain kept their secret to themselves.

It was a very great secret indeed—a state

secret—which none but so clever a man as the present King of Nomansland would ever have thought of. How he carried it out, undiscovered, I cannot tell. People said, long afterward, that it was by means of a gang of condemned criminals, who were set to work, and executed immediately after they had finished, so that nobody knew anything, or in the least suspected the real fact.

And what was the fact? Why, that this tower, which seemed a mere mass of masonry, utterly forsaken and uninhabited, was not so at all. Within twenty feet of the top some ingenious architect had planned a perfect little house, divided into four rooms—as by drawing a cross within a circle you will see might easily be done. By making skylights, and a few slits in the walls for windows, and raising a peaked roof which was hidden by the parapet, here was a dwelling complete, eighty feet from the ground, and as inaccessible as a rook's nest on the top of a tree.

A charming place to live in! if you once got up there—and never wanted to come down again.

Inside—though nobody could have looked inside except a bird, and hardly even a bird flew past that lonely tower—inside it was furnished with all the comfort and elegance imaginable; with lots of books and toys, and everything that the heart of a child could desire. For its only inhabitant, except a nurse of course, was a poor solitary child.

One winter's night, when all the plain was white with moonlight, there was seen crossing it a great tall black horse, ridden by a man also big and equally black, carrying before him on the saddle a woman and a child. The woman—she had a sad, fierce look, and no wonder, for she was a criminal under sentence of death, but her sentence had been changed to almost as severe a punishment. She was to inhabit the lonely tower with the child, and was allowed to live as long as the child lived—no longer. This in order that she might take the utmost care of him; for those who put him there were equally afraid of his dying and of his living.

Yet he was only a little, gentle boy, with a sweet, sleepy smile—he had been very tired from his long journey—and with clinging arms, which held tight to the man's neck, for he was rather frightened, and the face, black as it was, looked kindly at him. And he was very helpless, with his poor, small, shriveled legs, which could neither stand nor run away—for the little forlorn boy was Prince Dolor.

He had not been dead at all—or buried either. His grand funeral had been a mere pretense: a wax figure having been put in his place, while he himself was spirited away under charge of these two, the condemned woman and the black man. The latter was deaf and dumb, so could neither tell nor repeat anything.

When they reached the foot of the tower, there was light enough to see a huge chain dangling from the parapet, but dangling only halfway. The deaf-mute took from his saddle wallet a sort of ladder, arranged in pieces like a puzzle, fitted it together, and lifted it up to meet the chain. Then he mounted to the top of the tower, and slung from it a sort of chair, in which the woman and the child placed themselves and were drawn up, never to come down again as long as they lived. Leaving them there, the man descended the ladder, took it to pieces again and packed it in his pack, mounted the horse and disappeared across the plain.

Every month they used to watch for him, appearing like a speck in the distance. He fastened his horse to the foot of the tower, and climbed it, as before, laden with provisions and many other things. He always saw the Prince, so as to make sure that the child was alive and well, and then went away until the following month.

While his first childhood lasted, Prince Dolor was happy enough. He had every luxury that even a prince could need, and the one thing wanting—love—never having known, he did not miss. His nurse was very kind to him though she was a wicked woman. But either she had not been quite so wicked as people said, or she grew better through being shut up continually with a little innocent child who was dependent upon her for every comfort and pleasure of his life.

It was not an unhappy life. There was nobody to tease or ill-use him, and he was never ill. He played about from room to room—there were four rooms, parlor, kitchen, his nurse's bedroom, and his own; learned to crawl like a fly, and to jump like a frog, and to run about on all fours almost as fast as a puppy. In fact, he was very much like a puppy or a kitten, as thoughtless and as merry—scarcely ever cross, though sometimes a little weary.

As he grew older, he occasionally liked to be quiet for a while, and then he would sit at the slits of windows—which were, however, much bigger than they looked from the bottom of the tower—and watch the sky above and the ground below, with the storms sweeping over and the sunshine coming and going, and the shadows of the clouds running races across the blank plain.

By and by he began to learn lessons—not that his nurse had been ordered to teach him, but she did it partly to amuse herself. She was not a stupid woman, and Prince Dolor was by no means a stupid boy; so they got on very well, and his continual entreaty, "What can I do? what can you find me to do?" was stopped, at least for an hour or two in the day.

It was a dull life, but he had never know any other; anyhow, he remembered no other, and he did not pity himself at all. Not for a long time, till he grew quite a big little boy, and could read quite easily. Then he suddenly took to books, which the deaf-mute brought him from time to time—books which, not being acquainted with the literature of Nomansland, I cannot describe, but no doubt they were very interesting; and they informed him of everything in the outside world, and filled him with an intense longing to see it.

From this time a change came over the boy. He began to look sad and thin, and to shut himself up for hours without speaking. For his nurse hardly spoke, and whatever questions he asked beyond their ordinary daily life she never answered. She had, indeed, been forbidden, on pain of death, to tell him anything about himself, who he was, or what he might have been.

He knew he was Prince Dolor, because she always addressed him as "my prince" and "your Royal Highness," but what a prince was he had not the least idea. He had no idea of anything in the world, except what he found in his books.

He sat one day surrounded by them, having built them up round him like a little castle wall. He had been reading them half the day, but feeling all the while that to read about things which you never can see is like hearing about a beautiful dinner while you are starving. For almost the first time in his life he grew melancholy; his hands fell on his lap; he sat gazing out the window slit upon the view outside—the view he had looked at every day of his life, and might look at for endless days more.

Not a very cheerful view—just the plain and the sky—but he liked it. He used to think, if he could only fly out that window, up to the sky or down to the plain, how nice it would be! Perhaps when he died—his nurse had told him once in anger that he would never leave the tower till he died—he might be able to do this. Not that he understood much what dying meant, but it must be a change, and any change seemed to him a blessing.

"And I wish I had somebody to tell me about it—about that and many other things; somebody that would be fond of me, like my poor white kitten."

Here the tears came into his eyes, for the boy's one friend, the one interest of his life, had been a little white kitten, which the deaf-mute, kindly smiling, once took out of his pocket and gave him—the only living creature Prince Dolor had ever seen.

For four weeks it was his constant plaything and companion, till one moonlight night it took a fancy for wandering, climbed onto the parapet of the tower, dropped over and disappeared. It was not killed, he hoped, for cats had nine lives; indeed, he almost fancied he saw it pick itself up and scamper away; but he never caught sight of it again.

"Yes, I wish I had something better than a kitten—a person, a real live person, who would be fond of me and kind to me. Oh, I want somebody—dreadfully, dreadfully!"

As he spoke, there sounded behind him a slight tap-tap-tap, as of a stick or a cane, and twisting himself round, he saw—what do you think he saw?

Nothing either frightening or ugly, but still exceedingly curious. A little woman, no bigger than he might himself have been had his legs grown like those of other children; but she was not a child—she was an old woman. Her hair was gray, and her dress was gray, and there was a gray shadow over her wherever she moved. But she had the sweetest smile, the prettiest hands, and when she spoke it was in the softest voice imaginable.

"My dear little boy"—and dropping her cane, the only bright and rich thing about her, she laid those two tiny hands on his shoulders —"my own little boy, I could not come to you until you had said you wanted me; but now you do want me, her I am."

"And you are very welcome, madam," replied the Prince, trying to speak politely, as princes always did in books; "and I am exceedingly obliged to you. May I ask who you are? Perhaps my mother?" For he knew that little boys usually had a mother, and had occasionally wondered what had become of his own.

"No," said the visitor, with a tender, half-sad smile, putting back the hair from his forehead, and looking right into his eyes—"no, I am not your mother, though she was a dear friend of mine; and you are as like her as ever you can be."

"Will you tell her to come and see me, then?"

"She cannot; but I dare say she knows all about you. And she loves you very much—and so do I; and I want to help you all I can, my poor little boy."

"Why do you call me poor?" asked Prince Dolor, in surprise.

The little old woman glanced down on his legs and feet, which he did not know were different from those of other children, and then at his sweet, bright face, which, though he knew not that either, was exceedingly different from many children's faces, which are often so fretful, cross, sullen. Looking at him, instead of sighing, she smiled. "I beg your pardon, my Prince," said she.

"Yes, I am a prince, and my name is Dolor; will you tell me yours, madam?"

The little old woman laughed like a chime of silver bells.

"I have not got a name—or, rather, I have so many names that I don't know which to choose. However, it was I who gave you yours, and you will belong to me all your days. I am your godmother."

"Hurrah!" cried the little Prince; "I am glad I belong to you, for I like you very much. Will you come and play with me?"

So they sat down together and played. By and by they began to talk.

"Are you very dull here?" asked the little old woman.

"Not particularly, thank you, godmother. I have plenty to eat and drink, and my lessons to do, and my books to read—lots of books."

"And you want nothing?"

"Nothing. Yes—perhaps—If you please, godmother, could you bring me just one more thing?"

"What sort of thing?"

"A little boy to play with."

The old woman looked very sad. "Just the thing, alas! which I cannot give you. My child, I cannot alter your lot in any way, but I can help you to bear it."

"Thank you. But why do talk of bearing it? I have nothing to bear."

"My poor little man!" said the old woman in the very tenderest tone of her tender voice. "Kiss me!"

"What is kissing?" asked the wondering child.

His godmother took him in her arms and embraced him many times. By and by he kissed her back again—at first awkwardly and shyly, then with all the strength of his warm little heart.

"You are better to cuddle than even my white kitten, I think. Promise me that you will never go away."

"I must; but I will leave a present behind me —something as good as myself to amuse you— something that will take you wherever you want to go, and show you all that you wish to see."

"What is it?"

"A traveling cloak."

The Prince's countenance fell. "I don't want a cloak, for I never go out. Sometimes nurse hoists me onto the roof, and carries me round by the parapet; but that is all. I can't walk, you know, as she does."

"The more reason why you should ride; and besides, this traveling cloak—"

"Hush!—she's coming."

There sounded outside the room door a heavy step and a grumpy voice, and a rattle of plates and dishes.

"It's my nurse, and she is bringing my dinner; but I don't want dinner at all—I only want you. Will her coming drive you away, godmother?"

"Perhaps; but only for a little while. Never mind; all the bolts and bars in the world couldn't keep me out. I'd fly in at the window, or down through the chimney. Only wish for me, and I come.''

"Thank you," said Prince Dolor, but almost in a whisper, for he was very uneasy at what might happen next. His nurse and his godmother—what would they say to one another? how would they look at one another?—two such different faces: one harsh-lined, sullen, cross, and sad; the other sweet and bright and calm as a summer evening before the dark begins.

When the door was flung open, Prince Dolor shut his eyes, trembling all over. Opening them again, he saw he need fear nothing—his lovely old godmother had melted away just like the rainbow out of the sky, as he had watched it many a time. Nobody but his nurse was in the room.

"What a muddle your Royal Highness is sitting in," said she sharply. "Such a heap of untidy books; and what's this rubbish?" knocking a little bundle that lay beside them.

"Oh, nothing, nothing—give it me!" cried the Prince, and, darting after it, he hid it under his pinafore, and then pushed it quickly into his pocket. Rubbish as it was, it was left in the place where she sat, and might be something belonging to her—his dear, kind godmother, whom already he loved with all his lonely, tender, passionate heart.

It was, though he did not know this, his wonderful traveling cloak.

Chapter 4

And what of the traveling cloak? What sort of cloak was it, and what good did it do the Prince?

Stay, and I'll tell you all about it.

Outside it was the commonest-looking bundle imaginable —shabby and small; and the instant Prince Dolor touched it, it grew smaller still, dwindling down till he could put it in his trousers pocket, like a handkerchief rolled up into a ball. He did this at once, for fear his nurse should see it, and kept it there all day—all night, too. Till after his next morning's lessons he had no opportunity of examining his treasure.

When he did, it seemed no treasure at all; but a mere piece of cloth—circular in form, dark green in color—that is, if it had any color at all, being so worn and shabby, though not dirty. It had a split cut to the center, forming a roundhole for the neck—and that was all its shape; the shape, in fact, of those cloaks which in South America are called ponchos—very simple, but most graceful and convenient.

Prince Dolor had never seen anything like it. In spite of his disappointment, he examined it curiously. He spread it out on the floor, then arranged it on his shoulders. It felt very warm and comfortable; but it was so exceedingly shabby—the only shabby thing that the Prince had ever seen in his life.

"And what use will it be to me?" said he sadly. "I have no need of outdoor clothes, as I never go out. Why was this given to me? I wonder. And what in the world am I to do with it? She must be a rather funny person, this dear godmother of mine."

Nevertheless, because she was his godmother, and had given him the cloak, he folded it carefully and put it away, poor and shabby as it was, hiding it in a safe corner of his top cupboard, which his nurse never meddled with. He did not want her to find it, or to laugh at it or at his godmother—as he felt sure she would, if she knew all.

There it lay, and by and by he forgot all about it. Nay, I am sorry to say that, being a child, and not seeing her again, he almost forgot his sweet old godmother, or thought of her only as he did of angels or fairies that he read of in his books, and of her visit as if it had been a mere dream of the night.

There were times, certainly, when he recalled her: of early mornings, like that morning when she appeared beside him, and late evenings, when the gray twilight reminded him of the color of her hair color of her hair and her pretty soft garments; above all, when, waking in the middle of the night, with the stars peering in at his window, or the moonlight shining across his little bed he would not have been surprised to see her standing beside it, looking at him with those beautiful tender eyes, which seemed to have a pleasantness and comfort in them different from anything he had ever known.

But she never came, and gradually she slipped out of his memory—only a boy's memory, after all; until something happened which made him remember her, and want her as he had never wanted anything before.

Prince Dolor fell ill. He caught—his nurse could not tell how—a complaint common to the people of Nomansland, called the doldrums, as unpleasant as measles or any other of our complaints; and it made him restless, cross, and disagreeable. Even when a little better, he was to weak to enjoy anything, but lay all day long on his sofa, fidgeting his nurse extremely— while, in her intense terror lest he might die, she fidgeted him still more. At last, seeing he really was getting well, she left him to himself—which he was most glad of, in spite of his dullness and dreariness. There he lay, alone, quite alone.

Now and then an irritable fit came over him, in which he longed to get up and do something, or to go somewhere. He would have liked to imitate his white kitten—jump down from the tower and run away, taking the chance of whatever might happen.

Only one thing, alas! was likely to happen; for the kitten, he remembered, had four active legs, while he—

"I wonder what my godmother meant when she looked at my legs and sighed so bitterly? I wonder why I can't walk straight and steady like my nurse —only I wouldn't like to have her great, noisy, clumping shoes. Still it would be very nice to move about quickly—perhaps to fly, like a bird, like that string of birds I saw the other day skimming across the sky, one after the other."

These were the passage birds—the only living creatures that ever crossed the lonely plain; and he had been much interested in them, wondering whence they came and whither they were going.

"How nice it must be to be a bird! If legs are no good, why cannot one have wings? People have wings when they die—perhaps. I wish I were dead, that I do. I am so tired, so tired; and nobody cares for me. Nobody ever did care for me, except perhaps my godmother. Godmother, dear, have you quite forsaken me?"

He stretched himself wearily, gathered himself up, and dropped his head upon his hands; as he did so, he felt somebody kiss him on the back of his neck, and, turning, found that he was resting, not on the sofa pillows, but on a warm shoulder—that of the little old woman clothed in gray.

How glad he was to see her! How he looked into her kind eyes and felt her hands, to see if she were all real and alive! The he put both his arms round her neck, and kissed her as if he would never have done kissing.

"Stop, stop!" cried she, pretending to be smothered. "I see you have not forgotten my teachings. Kissing is a good thing—in moderation. Only just let me have breath to speak one word."

"A dozen!" he said.

"Well, then, tell me all that has happened to you since I saw you—or, rather, since you saw me, which is quite a different thing."

"Nothing has happened—nothing ever does happen to me," answered the Prince dolefully.

"And are you very dull, my boy?"

"So dull that I was just thinking whether I could not jump down to the bottom of the tower, like my white kitten."

"Don't do that, not being a white kitten."

"I wish I were—I wish I were anything but what I am."

"And you can't make yourself any different, nor can I do it either. You must be content to stay just what you are."

The little old woman said this—very firmly, but gently, too—with her arms round his neck and her lips on his forehead. It was the first time the boy had ever heard anyone talk like this, and he looked up in surprise—but not in pain, for her sweet manner softened the hardness of her words.

"Now, my Prince—for you are a prince, and must behave as such—let us see what we can do; how much I can do for you, or show you how to do for yourself. Where is your traveling cloak?"

Prince Dolor blushed extremely. "I—I put it away in the cupboard. I suppose it is there still."

"You have never used it; you dislike it?"

He hesitated, not wishing to be impolite. "Don't you think it's—just a little old and shabby for a prince?"

The old woman laughed—long and loud, though very sweetly.

"Prince, indeed! Why, if all the princes in the world craved for it, they couldn't get it, unless I gave it them. Old and shabby! It's the most valuable thing imaginable! Very few ever have it; but I thought I would give it to you, because—because you are different from other people."

"Am I?" said the Prince, and looked first with curiosity, then with a sort of anxiety, into his godmother's face, which was sad and grave, with slow tears beginning to steal down.

She touched his poor little legs. "These are not like those of other little boys."

"Indeed!—my nurse never told me that."

"Very likely not. But it is time you were told; and I tell you, because I love you."

"Tell me what, dear godmother?"

"That you will never be able to walk or run or jump or play—that your life will be quite different from most people's lives; but it may be a very happy life for all that. Do not be afraid."

"I am not afraid," said the boy. But he turned very pale, and his lips began to quiver, though he did not actually cry—he was too old for that, and, perhaps, too proud.

Though not wholly comprehending, he began dimly to guess what his godmother meant. He had never seen any real live boys, but he had seen pictures of them running and jumping; which he had admired and tried hard to imitate, but always failed. Now he began to understand why he failed, and that he always should fail—that, in fact, he was not like other little boys; and it was of no use his wishing to do as they did, and play as they played, even if he had had them to play with. His was a separate life, in which he must find out new work and new pleasures for himself.

The sense of *the inevitable,* as grown-up people call it—that we cannot have things as we want them to be but as they are, and that we must learn to bear them and make the best of them—this lesson, which everybody has to learn soon or late —came, alas! sadly soon to the poor boy. He fought against it for a while, and then, quite overcome, turned and sobbed bitterly in his godmother's arms.

She comforted him—I do not know how, except that love always comforts. And then she whispered to him, in her sweet, strong, cheerful voice: "Never mind!"

"No, I don't think I do mind—that is, I *won't* mind," replied he, catching the courage of her tone and speaking like a man, though he was still such a mere boy.

"That is right, my Prince!—that is being like a prince. Now we know exactly where we are; let us put our shoulders to the wheel and—"

"We are in Hopeless Tower [this was its name, if it had a name], and there is no wheel to put our shoulders to," said the child sadly.

"You little matter-of-fact goose! Well for you that you have a godmother called—"

"What?" he eagerly asked.

"Stuff-and-nonsense."

"Stuff-and-nonsense! What a funny name!"

"Some people give it me, but they are not my most intimate friends. These call me—never mind what," added the old woman, with a soft twinkle in her eyes. "So as you know me, and know me well, you may give me any name you please; it doesn't matter. But I am your godmother, child. I have few godchildren. Those I have love me dearly, and find me the greatest blessing in all the world."

"I can well believe it," cried the little lame Prince, and forgot his troubles in looking at her —as her figure dilated, her eyes grew lustrous as stars, her very raiment brightened, and the whole room seemed filled with her beautiful and beneficent presence like light.

He could have looked at her forever—half in love, half in awe; but she suddenly dwindled down into the little old woman all in gray, and, with a malicious twinkle in her eyes, asked for the traveling cloak.

"Bring it out of the rubbish cupboard, and shake the dust off it, quick!" said she to Prince Dolor, who hung his head, rather ashamed. "Spread it out on the floor, and wait till the split closes and the edges turn up like a rim all round. Then go and open the skylight—mind, I say *open the skylight*—set yourself down in the middle of it, like a frog on a water-lily leaf; say 'Abracadabra, dum dum dum,' and—see what will happen!"

The Prince burst into a fit of laughing. It all seemed so exceedingly silly; he wondered that a wise old woman like his godmother should talk such nonsense.

"Stuff-and-nonsense, you mean," said she, answering, to his great alarm, his unspoken thoughts. "Did I not tell you some people called me by that name? Never mind; it doesn't harm me."

And she laughed—her merry laugh—as child-like as if she were the Prince's age instead of her own, whatever that might be. She certainly was a most extraordinary old woman.

"Believe me or not, it doesn't matter," said she. "Here is the cloak. When you want to go traveling on it, say 'Abracadabra, dum dum dum'; when you want to come back again, say 'Abracadabra, tum tum ti.' That's all; good-by."

A puff of most pleasant air passing by him, making him feel for the moment quite strong and well, was all the Prince was conscious of. His most extraordinary godmother was gone.

"Really now, how rosy your Royal Highness's cheeks have grown! You seem to have got well already," said the nurse, entering the room.

"I think I have," replied the Prince very gently—he felt gentle and kind even to his grim nurse. "And now let me have my dinner, and go to your sewing as usual."

The instant she was gone, however, taking with her the plate and dishes, which for the first time since his illness he had satisfactorily cleared, Prince Dolor hopped down from his sofa, and with one or two of his froglike jumps reached the cupboard where he kept his toys, and looked everywhere for his traveling cloak.

Alas! it was not there.

While he was ill of the doldrums, his nurse, thinking it a good opportunity for putting things to rights, had made a grand clearance of all his "rubbish"—as she considered it. His beloved headless horse, broken carts, sheep without feet, and birds without wings—all the treasures of his

42

baby days, which he could not bear to part with, were gone. Though he seldom played with them now, he liked just to feel they were there.

They were all gone and with them the traveling cloak. He sat down on the floor, looking at the empty shelves, so beautifully clean and tidy, then burst out sobbing as if his heart would break.

But quietly—always quietly. He never let his nurse hear him cry. She only laughed at him, as he felt she would laugh now.

"And it is all my own fault!" he cried. "I ought to have taken better care of my godmother's gift. Oh, godmother, forgive me! I'll never be so careless again. I don't know what the cloak is exactly, but I am sure it is something precious. Help me find it again. Oh, don't let it be stolen from me—don't, please!"

"Ha, ha, ha!" laughed a silvery voice. "Why, that traveling cloak is the one thing in the world which nobody can steal. It is of no use to anybody except the owner. Open your eyes, my Prince, and see what you shall see."

His dear old godmother, he thought, and turned eagerly round. But no; he beheld, lying in a corner of the room, all dust and cobwebs, his precious traveling cloak.

Prince Dolor darted toward it, tumbling several times on the way, as he often did tumble, poor boy! and pick himself up again, never complaining. Snatching it to his breast, he hugged and kissed it, cobwebs and all, as if it had been something alive. Then he began unrolling it, wondering each minute what would happen. What did happen was so curious that I must leave it for another chapter.

Chapter 5

If any reader, big or little, should wonder whether there is a meaning in this story deeper than that of an ordinary fairy tale, I will own that there is. But I have hidden it so carefully that the smaller people, and many larger folk, will never find it out, and meantime the book may be read straight on, like *Cinderella*, or *Bluebeard*, or *Hop-o'My-Thumb*, for what interest it has or what amusement it may bring.

Having said this, I return to Prince Dolor, that little lame boy whom many may think so exceedingly to be pitied. But if you had seen him as he sat patiently untying his wonderful cloak, which was done up in a very tight and perplexing parcel, using skillfully his deft little hands, and knitting his brows with firm determination, while his eyes glistened with pleasure and energy and eager anticipation—if you had beheld him thus, you might have changed your opinion.

When we see people suffering or unfortunate, we feel very sorry for them. But when we see them bravely bearing their sufferings and making the best of their misfortunes, it is quite a different thing. We respect, we admire them. One can respect and admire even a little child.

When Prince Dolor had patiently untied all the knots, a remarkable thing happened. The cloak began to undo itself. Slowly unfolding, it laid itself down on the carpet, as flat as if it had been ironed. The split joined with a little sharp crick-crack, and the rim turned up all round till it was breast-high. Meantime the cloak had grown and grown, and become quite large enough for one person to sit in it as comfortably as if in a boat.

The Prince watched it rather anxiously; it was such an extraordinary, not to say frightening, thing. However, he was no coward, but a thorough boy, who, if he had been like other boys, would doubtless have grown up daring and adventurous—a soldier, a sailor, or the like. As it was, he could only show his courage morally, not physically, by being afraid of nothing, and by doing boldly all that it was in his narrow powers to do. And I am not sure but that in this way he showed more real valor than if he had had six pairs of proper legs.

He said to himself: "What a goose I am! As if my dear godmother would ever have given me anything to hurt me. Here goes!"

So, with one of his active leaps, he sprang right into the middle of the cloak, where he squatted down, wrapping his arms tight round his knees, for they shook a little and his heart beat fast. But there he sat, steady and silent, waiting for what might happen next.

Nothing did happen, and he began to think nothing would, and to feel rather disappointed, when he recollected the words he had been told to repeat—"Abracadabra, dum dum dum!"

He repeated them, laughing all the while, they seemed such nonsense. And then—and then—

Now I don't expect anybody to believe what I am going to relate, though a good many wise people have believed a good many sillier things. And as seeing's believing, and I never saw it, I cannot be expected implicitly to believe it myself, except in a sort of way. And yet there is truth in it—for some people.

The cloak rose, slowly and steadily, at first only a few inches, then gradually higher and higher, till it nearly touched the skylight. Prince Dolor's head actually bumped against the glass, or would have done so had he not crouched down, crying, "Oh, please don't hurt me!" in a most melancholy voice.

Then he suddenly remembered his godmother's express command—"Open the skylight!"

Regaining his courage at once, without a moment's delay he lifted up his head and began searching for the bolt—the cloak meanwhile remaining perfectly still, balanced in the air. But the minute the window was opened, out it sailed—right out into the clear, fresh air, with nothing between it and the cloudless blue.

Prince Dolor had never felt any such delicious sensation before. I can understand it. Cannot you? Did you never think, in watching the rooks going home singly or in pairs, soaring their way across the calm evening sky till they vanish like black dots in the misty gray, how pleasant it must feel to be up there, quite out of the noise and din of the world, able to hear and see everything down below, yet troubled by nothing and teased by no one—all alone, but perfectly content?

Something like this was the happiness of the little lame Prince when he got out of Hopeless Tower, and found himself for the first time in the pure open air, with the sky above him and the earth below.

True, there was nothing but earth and sky; no houses, no trees, no rivers, mountains, seas—not a beast on the ground or a bird in the air. But to him even the level plain looked beautiful. And then there was the glorious arch of the sky, with a little young moon sitting in the west like a baby queen. And the evening breeze was so sweet and fresh—it kissed him like his godmother's kisses. And by and by a few stars came out—first two or three, and then quantities—quantities! so that when he began to count them he was utterly bewildered.

By this time, however, the cool breeze had become cold. The mist gathered; and as he had, as he said, no outdoor clothes, poor Prince Dolor was not very comfortable. The dews fell damp on his curls. He began to shiver.

"Perhaps I had better go home," thought he.

But how? For in his excitement the other words which his godmother had told him to use had slipped his memory. They were only a little different from the first, but in that slight difference all the importance lay. As he repeated his "Abraca-dabra," trying ever so many other syllables after it, the cloak only went faster and faster, skimming on through the dusky, empty air.

The poor little Prince began to feel frightened. What if this wonderful traveling cloak should keep on thus traveling, perhaps to the world's end, carrying with it a poor, tired, hungry boy, who, after all, was beginning to think there was something very pleasant in supper and bed!

"Dear godmother," he cried pitifully, "do help me! Tell me just this once and I'll never forget again."

Instantly the words came rushing into his head—"Abracadabra, tum tum ti!" Was that it? Ah! yes—for the cloak began to turn slowly. He repeated the charm again, more distinctly and firmly, when it gave a gentle dip, like a nod of satisfaction, and immediately started back, as fast as ever, in the direction of the tower.

He reached the skylight, which he found exactly as he had left it, and slipped in, cloak and all, as easily as he had got out. He had scarcely reached the floor, and was still sitting in the middle of his traveling cloak—like a frog on a water-lily leaf, as his godmother had expressed it—when he heard his nurse's voice outside.

"Bless us! what has become of your Royal Highness all this time? To sit stupidly here at the window till it is quite dark, and leave the skylight open, too. Prince! what can you be thinking of? You are the silliest boy I ever knew."

"Am I?" said he absently, and never heeding her crossness; for his only anxiety was lest she might find out what he had been doing.

She would have been a very clever person to have done so. The instant Prince Dolor got off it, the cloak folded itself up into the tiniest possible parcel, tied all its own knots, and rolled itself of its own accord into the farthest and darkest corner of the room. If the nurse had seen it, which she didn't, she would have taken it for a mere bundle of rubbish not worth noticing.

Shutting the skylight with an angry bang, she brought in the supper and lit the candles with her usual unhappy expression of countenance. But Prince Dolor hardly saw it. He saw only, hid in the corner where nobody else would see it, his wonderful traveling cloak. And though his supper was not particularly nice, he ate it heartily, scarcely hearing a word of his nurse's grumbling, which tonight seemed to have taken the place of her sullen silence.

"Poor woman!" he thought, when he paused a minute to listen and look at her with those quiet, happy eyes, so like his mother's. "Poor woman! she hasn't got a traveling cloak!"

And when he was left alone at last, and crept into his little bed, where he lay awake a good while, watching what he called his "sky-garden," all planted with stars, like flowers, his chief thought was—"I must be up very early tomorrow morning, and get my lessons done, and then I'll go traveling all over the world on my beautiful cloak."

So the next day he opened his eyes with the sun, and went with a good heart to his lessons. They had hitherto been the chief amusement of his dull life. Now, I am afraid, he found them also a little dull. But he tried to be good—I don't say Prince Dolor always was good, but he generally tried to be—and when his mind went wandering after the dark, dusty corner where lay his precious treasure, he resolutely called it back again.

"For," he said, "how ashamed my godmother would be of me if I grew up a stupid boy!"

But the instant lessons were done, and he was alone in the empty room, he crept across the floor, undid the shabby little bundle, his fingers trembling with eagerness, climbed on the chair, and thence to the table, so as to unbar the skylight—he forgot nothing now—said his magic charm, and was away out the window, as children say, "in a few minutes less than no time."

Nobody missed him. He was accustomed to sit so quietly always that his nurse, though only in the next room, perceived no difference. And besides, she might have gone in and out a dozen times, and it would have been just the same; she never could have found out his absence.

For what do you think the clever godmother did? She took a quantity of moonshine, or some equally convenient material, and made an image, which she set on the windowsill reading, or by the table drawing, where it looked so like Prince Dolor that any common observer would never had guessed the deception. And even the boy would have been puzzled to know which was the image and which was himself.

And all this while the happy little fellow was away, floating in the air on his magic cloak, and seeing all sorts of wonderful things—or they seemed wonderful to him, who had hitherto seen nothing at all.

First, there were the flowers that grew on the plain, which, whenever the cloak came near enough, he strained his eyes to look at. They were very tiny, but very beautiful—white saxifrage, and yellow lotus, and ground thistles, purple and bright, with many others the names of which I do not know. No more did Prince Dolor, though he tried to find them out by recalling any pictures he had seen of them. But he was too far off; and though it was pleasant enough to admire them as brilliant patches of color, still he would have liked to examine them all. He was, as a little girl I know once said of a playfellow, "a very examining boy."

"I wonder," he thought, "whether I could see better through a pair of glasses like those my nurse reads with, and takes such care of. How I would take care of them, too, if I only had a pair!"

Immediately he felt something queer and hard fixing itself to the bridge of his nose. It was a pair of the prettiest gold spectacles ever seen. Looking downward, he found that, though ever so high above the ground, he could see every minute blade of grass, every tiny bud and flower—nay, even the insects that walked over them.

"Thank you, thank you!" he cried, in a gush of gratitude—to anybody or everybody, but especially to his dear godmother, who he felt sure had given him this new present. He amused himself with it for ever so long, with his chin pressed on the rim of the cloak, gazing down upon the grass, every square foot of which was a mine of wonders.

Then, just to rest his eyes, he turned them up to

the sky—the blue, bright, empty sky, which he had looked at so often and seen nothing.

Now surely there was something. A long, black, wavy line, moving on in the distance, not by chance, as the clouds move apparently, but deliberately, as if it were alive. He might have seen it before—he almost thought he had; but then he could not tell what it was. Looking at it through his spectacles, he discovered that it really was alive; being a long string of birds, flying one after the other, their wings moving steadily and their heads pointed in one direction, as steadily as if each were a little ship, guided invisibly by an unerring helm.

"They must be the passage birds flying seaward!" cried the boy, who had read a little about them, and had a great talent for putting two and two together and finding out all he could. "Oh, how I should like to see them quite close, and to know where they come from and whither they are going! How I wish I knew everything in all the world!"

A silly speech for even an "examining" little boy to make; because, as we grow older, the more we know the more we find out there is to know. And Prince Dolor blushed when he had said it, and hoped nobody had heard him.

Apparently somebody had, however. For the cloak gave a sudden bound forward, and presently he found himself high in the air, in the very middle of that band of aerial travelers, who had no magic cloak to travel on—nothing except their wings. Yet there they were, making their fearless way through the sky.

Prince Dolor looked at them as one after the

other they glided past him; and they looked at him—those pretty swallows with their changing necks and bright eyes—as if wondering to meet in mid-air such an extraordinary sort of bird.

"Oh, I wish I were going with you, you lovely creatures! I'm so tired of this dull plain, and the dreary and lonely tower. I do so want to see the world! Pretty swallows, dear swallows! tell me what it looks like—the beautiful, wonderful world!"

But the swallows flew past him—steadily, slowly pursuing their course as if inside each little head had been a mariner's compass, to guide him safe over land and sea, direct to the place where he wished to go.

The boy looked after them with envy. For a long time he followed with his eyes the faint, wavy black line as it floated away, sometimes changing its curves a little, but never deviating from its settled course, till it vanished entirely out of sight.

Then he settled himself down in the center of the cloak, feeling quite sad and lonely.

"I think I'll go home," said he, and repeated his "Abracadabra, tum tum ti!" with a rather heavy heart. The more he had, the more he wanted. It is not always one can have everything one wants—at least, at the exact minute one craves for it; not even though one is a prince, and has a powerful and beneficent godmother.

He did not like to vex her by calling for her and telling her how unhappy he was, in spite of all her goodness. So he just kept his trouble to himself, went back to his lonely tower, and spent three days in silent melancholy, without even attempting another journey on his traveling cloak.

Chapter 6

The fourth day it happened that the deaf-mute paid his accustomed visit, after which Prince Dolor's spirits rose. They always did when he got the new books which, just to relieve his conscience, the King of Nomansland regularly sent to his nephew; with many new toys also, though the latter were disregarded now.

"Toys, indeed! when I'm a big boy," said the Prince, with disdain, and would scarcely condescend to mount a rocking horse which had come, somehow or other—I can't be expected to explain things very exactly—packed on the back of the other, the great black horse, which stood and fed contentedly at the bottom of the tower.

Prince Dolor leaned over and looked at it, and thought how grand it must be to get upon its back—this grand live steed—and ride away, like the pictures of knights.

"Suppose I were a knight," he said to himself; "then I should be obliged to ride out and see the world."

But he kept all these thoughts to himself, and just sat still, devouring his new books till he had come to the end of them all. It was a repast not unlike the Barmecide feast which you read of in the *Arabian Nights*, which consisted of very elegant but empty dishes, or that supper of Sancho Panza in *Don Quixote*, where, the minute the smoking dishes came on the table, the physician waved his hand and they were all taken away.

Thus almost all the ordinary delights of boy life had been taken away from, or rather never given to, this poor little prince.

"I wonder," he would sometimes think—"I wonder what it feels like to be on the back of a horse, galloping away, or holding the reins in a carriage, and tearing across the country, or jumping a ditch, or running a race, such as I read of or see in pictures. What a lot of things there are that I should like to do! But first I should like to go and see the world. I'll try."

Apparently it was his godmother's plan always to let him try, and try hard, before he gained anything. This day the knots that tied up his traveling cloak were more than usually troublesome, and he was a full half hour before he got out into the open air, and found himself floating merrily over the top of the tower.

Hitherto, in all his journeys, he had never let himself go out of sight of home, for the dreary building, after all, was home—he remembered no other. But now he felt sick of the very look of his tower, with its round smooth walls and level battlements.

"Off we go!" cried he, when the cloak stirred itself with a slight, slow motion, as if awaiting his orders. "Anywhere—anywhere, so that I am away from here, and out into the world."

As he spoke, the cloak, as if seized suddenly with a new idea, bounded forward and went skimming through the air, faster than the very fastest railway train.

"Gee-up! gee-up!" cried Prince Dolor in great excitement. "This is as good as riding a race."

And he patted the cloak as if it had been a horse—that is, in the way he supposed horses ought to be patted—and tossed his head back to meet the fresh breeze, and pulled his coat collar up and his hat down as he felt the wind grow keener and colder—colder than anything he had ever known.

"What does it matter, though?" said he. "I'm a boy, and boys ought not to mind anything."

Still, for all his good will, by and by, he began to shiver exceedingly. Also, he had come away without his dinner, and he grew frightfully hungry. And to add to everything, the sunshiny day changed into rain, and being high up, in the very midst of the clouds, he got soaked through and through in a very few minutes.

"Shall I turn back?" meditated he. "Suppose I say 'Abracadabra'?"

Here he stopped, for already the cloak gave an obedient lurch, as if it were expecting to be sent home immediately.

"No—I can't—I can't go back! I must go forward and see the world. But oh! if I had but the shabbiest old rug to shelter me from the rain, or the driest morsel of bread and cheese, just to keep me from starving! Still, I don't much mind. I'm a prince, and ought to be able to stand anything. Hold on, cloak, we'll make the best of it."

It was a most curious circumstance, but no sooner had he said this than he felt stealing over his knees something warm and soft; in fact, a most beautiful bearskin, which folded itself round him quite naturally, and cuddled him up as closely as if he had been the cub of the kind old mother bear that once owned it. Then feeling in his pocket, which suddenly stuck out in a marvelous way, he found, not exactly bread and cheese, nor even sandwiches, but a packet of the most delicious food he had ever tasted. It was not meat, nor pudding, but a combination of both, and it served him excellently for both. He ate his dinner with the greatest gusto imaginable, till he grew so thirsty he did not know what to do.

"Couldn't I have just one drop of water, if it didn't trouble you too much, kindest of god-mothers?"

For he really thought this want was beyond her power to supply. All the water which supplied Hopeless Tower was pumped up with difficulty from a deep artesian well—there were such things known in Nomansland—which had been drilled at the foot of it. But around, for miles upon miles, the desolate plain was per-fectly dry. And above it, high in the air, how could he expect to find a well, or to get even a drop of water?

He forgot one thing—the rain. While he spoke, it came on in another wild burst, as if the clouds had poured themselves out in a passion of crying, wetting him certainly, but leaving behind, in a large glass vessel which he had never noticed before, enough water to quench the thirst of two or three boys at least. And it was so fresh, so pure—as water from the clouds always is when it does not catch the soot from city chimneys and other defilements—that he drank it, every drop, with the greatest delight and content.

Also, as soon as it was empty the rain filled it again, so that he was able to wash his face and hands and refresh himself exceedingly. Then the sun came out and dried him in no time. After that he curled himself up under the bearskin rug, and though he determined to be the most wide-awake boy imaginable, being so snug and warm and comfortable, Prince Dolor condescended to shut his eyes just for one minute. The next minute he was sound asleep.

When he awoke, he found himself floating over a country quite unlike anything he had ever seen before.

Yet it was nothing but what most of you children see every day and never notice it—a pretty country landscape, like England, Scotland, America, or any other land you choose to name. It had no particular features—nothing in it was grand or lovely. It was simply pretty, nothing more. Yet to Prince Dolor, who had never gone beyond his lonely tower and level plain, it appeared the most charming sight imaginable.

First, there was a river. It came tumbling

down the hillside, frothing and foaming, playing at hide-and-seek among the rocks, then bursting out in noisy fun like a child, to bury itself in deep, still pools. Afterward it went steadily on for a while, like a good grown-up person, till it came to another big rock, where it misbehaved itself extremely. It turned into a cataract, and went tumbling over and over, after a fashion that made the Prince —who had never seen water before, except in his bath or drinking cup—clap his hands with delight.

"It is so active, so alive! I like things active and alive!" cried he, and watched it shimmering and dancing, whirling and leaping, till, after a few windings and vagaries, it settled into a respectable stream. After that it went along, deep and quiet, but flowing steadily on, till it reached a large lake, into which it slipped and so ended its course.

All this the boy saw, either with his own naked eyes or through his gold spectacles. He saw also as in a picture, beautiful but silent, many other things which struck him with wonder, especially a grove of trees.

Only think, to have lived to his age (which he himself did not know, as he did not know his own birthday) and never to have seen trees! As he floated over these oaks, they seemed to him—trunk, branches, and leaves—the most curious sight imaginable.

"If I could only get nearer, so as to touch them," said he, and immediately the obedient cloak ducked down. Prince Dolor made a snatch at the topmost twig of the tallest tree, and caught a bunch of leaves in his hand.

Just a bunch of green leaves—such as we see

in myriads; watching them bud, grow, fall, and then kicking them along on the ground as if they were worth nothing. Yet how wonderful they are—every one of them a little different. I don't suppose you could ever find two leaves exactly alike in form, color, and size—no more than you could find two faces alike, or two characters exactly the same. The plan of this world is infinite similarity and yet infinite variety.

Prince Dolor examined his leaves with the greatest curiosity—and also a little caterpillar that he found walking over one of them. He coaxed it to take an additional walk over his finger, which it did with the greatest dignity and decorum, as if it, Mr. Caterpillar, were the most important individual in existence. It amused him for a long time; when a sudden gust of wind blew it overboard, leaves and all, he felt quite disconsolate.

"Still there must be many live creatures in the world besides caterpillars. I should like to see a few of them."

The cloak gave a little dip down, as if to say "All right, my Prince," and bore him across the oak forest to a long fertile valley—called in Scotland a strath and in England a weald, but what they call it in the tongue of Nomansland I do not know. It was made up of cornfields, pasturefields, lanes, hedges, brooks, and ponds. Also, in it were what the Prince desired to see—a quantity of living creatures, wild and tame. Cows and horses, lambs and sheep, fed in the meadows; pigs and fowls walked about the farmyards; and in lonelier places hares scudded, rabbits burrowed, and pheasants and partridges, with many other smaller birds, inhabited the fields and woods.

Through his wonderful spectacles the Prince could see everything. But, as I said, it was a silent picture; he was too high up to catch anything except a faint murmur, which only aroused his anxiety to hear more.

"I have as good as two pairs of eyes," he thought. "I wonder if my godmother would give me a second pair of ears."

Scarcely had he spoken that he found lying on his lap the most curious little parcel, all done up in silvery paper. And it contained—what do you think? Actually a pair of silver ears, which, when he tried them on, fitted so exactly over his own that he hardly felt them, except for the difference they made in his hearing.

There is something which we listen to daily and never notice. I mean the sounds of the visible world, animate and inanimate. Winds blowing, waters flowing, trees stirring, insects whirring (dear me! I am quite unconsciously writing rhyme), with the various cries of birds and beasts—lowing cattle, bleating sheep, grunting pigs, and cackling hens—all the infinite discords that somehow or other make a beautiful harmony.

We hear this, and are so accustomed to it that we think nothing of it. But Prince Dolor, who had lived all his days in the dead silence of Hopeless Tower, heard it for the first time. And oh! if you had seen his face.

He listened, listened, as if he could never

have done listening. And he looked and looked, as if he could not gaze enough. Above all, the motion of the animals delighted him: cows walking, horse galloping, little lambs and calves running races across the meadows, were such a treat for him to watch—he that was always so quiet. But, these creatures having four legs, and he only two, the difference did not strike him painfully.

Still, by and by, after the fashion of children —and, I fear, of many big people too—he began to want something more than he had, something fresh and new.

"Godmother," he said, having now begun to believe that, whether he saw her or not, he could always speak to her with full confidence that she would hear him—"godmother, all these creatures I like exceedingly; but I should like better to see a creature like myself. Couldn't you show me just one little boy?"

There was a sigh behind him—it might have been only the wind—and the cloak remained so long balanced motionless in air that he was half afraid his godmother had forgotten him, or was offended with him asking too much. Suddenly a shrill whistle startled him, even through his silver ears, and looking downward, he saw start up from behind a bush on a common, something—

Neither a sheep nor a horse nor a cow—nothing upon four legs. This creature had only two; but they were long, straight, and strong. And it had a lithe, active body, and a curly head of black hair set upon its shoulders. It was a boy, a shepherd boy, about the Prince's own age—but, oh! so different.

Not that he was an ugly boy—though his face was almost as red as his hands, and his shaggy hair matted like the backs of his own sheep. He was rather a nice-looking lad; and seemed so bright and healthy and good-tempered— "jolly" would be the word, only I am not sure if they have such a one in the elegant language of Nomansland—that the little Prince watched him with great admiration.

"Might he come and play with me? I would drop down to the ground to him, or fetch him up to me here. Oh, how nice it would be if I only had a little boy to play with me."

But the cloak, usually so obedient to his wishes, disobeyed him now. There were evidently some things which his godmother either could not or would not give. The cloak hung stationary, high in air, never attempting to descend. The shepherd lad evidently took it for a large bird, and, shading his eyes, looked up at it, making the Prince's heart beat fast.

However, nothing ensued. The boy turned round, with a long, loud whistle—seemingly his usual and only way of expressing his feelings. He could not make the thing out exactly—it was rather a mysterious affair, but it did not trouble him much—he was not an "examining" boy.

Then, stretching himself, for he had been evidently half asleep, he began flopping his shoulders with his arms to wake and warm himself; while his dog, a rough collie, who had been guarding the sheep meanwhile, began to jump upon him, barking with delight.

"Down, Snap, down! Stop that, or I'll thrash you," the Prince heard him say; though with such a rough voice and queer pronunciation that it was difficult to make the words out. "Hollo! Let's warm ourselves by a race."

They started off, boy and dog—barking and shouting, till it was doubtful which made the more noise or ran the faster. A regular steeplechase it was: first across the level common, greatly disturbing the quiet sheep; and then tearing away across country, scrambling through hedges and leaping ditches, and tumbling up and down over plowed fields. They did not seem to have anything to run for—but they ran as if they did it, both of them, for the mere pleasure of motion.

And what a pleasure that seemed! To the dog of course, but scarcely less so to the boy. How he skimmed along over the ground—his cheeks glowing, and his hair flying, and his legs—oh, what a pair of legs he had!

Prince Dolor watched him with great intentness, and in a state of excitement almost equal to that of the runner himself—for a while. Then the sweet, pale face grew a trifle paler, the lips began to quiver, and the eyes to fill.

"How nice it must be to run like that!" he said softly, thinking that never—no, never in this world—would he be able to do the same.

Now he understood what his godmother had meant when she gave him his traveling cloak, and why he had heard that sigh—he was sure it was hers—when he had asked to see "just one little boy."

"I think I had rather not look at him again," said the poor little Prince, drawing himself back into the center of his cloak, and resuming his favorite posture, sitting like a Turk, with his arms wrapped round his feeble, useless legs.

"You're no good to me," he said, patting them mournfully. "You never will be any good to me. I wonder why I had you at all. I wonder why I was born at all, since I was not to grow up like other boys. Why not?"

A question so strange, so sad, yet so often occurring in some form or other in this world—as you will find, my children, when you are older—that even if he had put it to his mother she could only have answered it, as we have to answer many as difficult things, by simply saying, "I don't know." There is much that we do not know and cannot understand—we big folks any more than you little ones. We have to accept it all just as you have to accept anything which your parents may tell you, even though you don't as yet see the reason of it. You may sometime, if you do exactly as they tell you, and are content to wait.

Prince Dolor sat a good while thus, or it appeared to him a good while, so many thoughts came and went through his poor young mind—thoughts of great bitterness, which, little though he was, seemed to make him grow years older in a few minutes.

Then he fancied the cloak began to rock gently to and fro, with a soothing kind of motion, as if he were in somebody's arms, somebody who did not speak, but loved him and comforted him without need of words. Not by deceiving him with false encouragement or hope, but by making him see the plain, hard truth in all its hardness, and thus letting him quietly face it, till it became softened, and did not seem nearly so dreadful after all.

Through the dreary silence and blankness, for he had placed himself so that he could see nothing but the sky, and had taken off his silver ears as well as his gold spectacles—what was the use of either when he had no legs with which to walk or run?—up from below there rose a delicious sound.

You have heard it hundreds of times, my children, and so have I. When I was a child I thought there was nothing so sweet; and I think so still. It was just the song of a skylark, mounting higher and higher from the ground, till it came so close that Prince Dolor could distinguish its quivering wings and tiny body, almost too tiny to contain such a gush of music.

"Oh, you beautiful, beautiful bird!" cried he; "I should dearly like to take you in and cuddle you. That is, if I could—if I dared."

But he hesitated. The little brown creature with its loud heavenly voice almost made him afraid. Nevertheless, it also made him happy. And he watched and listened—so absorbed that he forgot all regret and pain, forgot everything in the world except the little lark.

It soared and soared, and he was just wondering if it would soar out of sight, and what in the world he should do when it was gone, when it suddenly closed its wings, as larks do when they mean to drop to the ground. But, instead of dropping to the ground, it dropped right onto the little boy's breast.

What felicity! If it would only stay! A tiny, soft thing to fondle and kiss, to sing to him all day long and be his playfellow and companion, tame and tender, while to the rest of the world it was a wild bird of the air. What a pride, what a delight! To have something that nobody else had—something all his own. As the traveling cloak traveled on, he little heeded where, and the lark still stayed, nestled down in his bosom, hopped from his hand to his shoulder, and kissed him with its dainty beak, as if it loved him. Prince Dolor forgot all his grief, and was entirely happy.

But when he got in sight of Hopeless Tower a painful thought struck him.

"My pretty bird, what am I to do with you? If I take you into my room and shut you up there, you, a wild skylark of the air, what will become of you? I am used to this, but you are not. You will be so miserable. And suppose my nurse should find you—she who can't bear the sound of singing? Besides, I remember her once telling me that the nicest thing she ever ate in her life was a lark pie!"

The little boy shivered all over at the thought. And, though the merry lark immediately broke into the loudest carol, as if saying derisively that he defied anybody to eat him, still Prince Dolor was very uneasy. In another minute he had made up his mind.

"No, my bird, nothing so dreadful shall

happen to you if I can help it. I would rather do without you altogether. Yes, I'll try. Fly away, my darling, my beautiful! Good-by, my merry, merry bird.''

Opening his two caressing hands, in which, as if for protection, he had folded it, he let the lark go. It lingered a minute, perching on the rim of the cloak, and looking at him with eyes of almost human tenderness. Then away it flew, far up into the blue sky. It was only a bird.

But some time afterward, when Prince Dolor had eaten his supper—somewhat drearily, except for the thought that he could not possibly sup off lark pie now—and gone quietly to bed, the old familiar little bed, where he was accustomed to sleep, or lie awake contentedly thinking—suddenly he heard outside the window a little faint carol—faint but cheerful—cheerful even though it was the middle of the night.

The dear little lark! it had not flown away, after all. And it was truly the most extraordinary bird, for, unlike ordinary larks, it kept hovering about the tower in the silence and darkness of the night, outside the window or over the roof. Whenever he listened for a moment, he heard it singing still.

He went to sleep as happy as a king.

Chapter 7

"Happy as a king." How far kings are happy I cannot say, no more than could Prince Dolor, though he had once been a king himself. But he remembered nothing about it, and there was nobody to tell him, except his nurse, who had been forbidden upon pain of death to let him know anything about his dead parents, or the King his uncle, or indeed any part of his own history.

Sometimes he speculated about himself, whether he had had a father and mother as other little boys had, what they had been like, and why he had never seen them. But, knowing nothing about them, he did not miss them— only once or twice, reading pretty stories about little children and their mothers, who helped them when they were in difficulty and comforted them when they were sick, he, feeling ill and dull and lonely, wondered what had become of his mother and why she never came to see him.

Then, in his history lessons, of course, he read about kings and princes, and the government of different countries, and the events that happened there. And though he but faintly took in all this, still he did take in a little, and worried his young brain about it, and perplexed his nurse with questions, to which she returned sharp and mysterious answers, which only set him thinking the more.

He had plenty of time for thinking. After his last journey which had given him so much pain, his desire to see the world somehow faded away. He contented himself with reading his books, and looking out the tower windows, and listening to his beloved little lark, which had come home with him that day, and had never left him again.

True, it kept out of the way; and though his nurse sometimes dimly heard it, and said, "What is that horrid noise outside?" she never got the faintest chance of making it into a lark pie. Prince Dolor had his pet all to himself, and though he seldom saw it, he knew it was near him, and he caught continually, at odd hours of the day, and even in the night, fragments of its delicious song.

All during the winter—so far as there ever was any difference between summer and winter in Hopeless Tower—the little bird cheered and amused him. He scarcely needed anything more —not even his traveling cloak, which lay bundled up unnoticed in a corner, tied up in its innumerable knots.

Nor did his godmother come near him. It seemed as if she had given these treasures and left him alone—to use them or lose them, apply them or misapply them, according to his own choice.

That is all we can do with children when they grow into big children old enough to distinguish between right and wrong, and too old to be forced to do either.

Prince Dolor was now quite a big boy. Not tall—alas! he never could be that, with his poor little shrunken legs, which were of no use, only an encumbrance. But he was stout and strong, with great sturdy shoulders, and muscular arms, upon which he could swing himself about almost like a monkey. As if in compensation for his useless lower limbs, Nature had given to these extra strength and activity. His face, too, was very handsome. It was thinner, firmer, more manly; but still the sweet face of his childhood—his mother's own face.

How his mother would have liked to look at him! Perhaps she did—who knows?

The boy was not a stupid boy either. He could learn almost anything he chose—and he did choose, which was more than half the battle. He never gave up his lessons till he had learned them all—never thought it a punishment that he had to work at them, and that they cost him a deal of trouble sometimes.

"But," thought he, "men work, and it must be so grand to be a man—a prince too; and I fancy princes work harder than anybody—except kings. The princes I read about generally turn into kings. I wonder—" the boy was always wondering. "Nurse"—and one day he startled her with a sudden question—"tell me— shall I ever be a king?"

The woman stood, perplexed beyond expression. So long a time had passed by since her crime—if it were a crime—and her sentence that she now seldom thought of either. Even her punishment—to be shut up for life in Hopeless Tower —she had gradually got used to. Used also to the little lame Prince, her charge—whom at first she had hated, though she carefully did everything to keep him alive, since upon him her own life hung.

But latterly she had ceased to hate him, and, in a sort of way, almost loved him—at least, enough to be sorry for him—an innocent child, imprisoned here till he grew into an old man, and became a dull, worn-out creature like herself. Sometimes, watching him, she felt more sorry for him than even for herself; and then, seeing she looked a less miserable and ugly woman, he did not shrink from her as usual.

He did not now. "Nurse—dear nurse," said he, "I don't mean to vex you, but tell me—what is a king? Shall I ever be one?"

When she began to think less of herself and more of the child, the woman's courage increased. The idea came to her—what harm would it be, even if he did know his own history? Perhaps he ought to know it—for there had been various ups and downs, usurpations, revolutions, and restorations in Nomansland, as in most other countries. Something might happen—who could tell? Changes might occur. Possibly a crown would even yet be set upon those pretty, fair curls— which she began to think prettier than ever when she saw the imaginary coronet upon them.

She sat down, considering whether her oath, never to "say a word" to Prince Dolor about himself, would be broken if she were to take a pencil and write what was to be told. A mere quibble—a mean, miserable quibble. But then she was a miserable woman, more to be pitied than scorned.

After long doubt, and with great trepidation, she put her fingers to her lips, and taking the Prince's slate—with the sponge tied to it, ready to rub out the writing in a minute—she wrote:

"You are a king."

Prince Dolor started. His face grew pale, and then flushed all over; he held himself erect. Lame as he was, anybody could see he was born to be a king.

"Hush!" said the nurse, as he was beginning to speak. And then, terribly frightened all the while —people who have done wrong always are frightened—she wrote down in a few hurried sentences his history. How his parents had died—his uncle had usurped his throne, and sent him to end his days in this lonely tower.

"I, too," added she, bursting into tears. "Unless, indeed, you could get out into the world, and fight for your rights like a man. And fight for me also, my Prince, that I may not die in this desolate place."

"Poor old nurse!" said the boy compassionately. For somehow, boy as he was, when he heard he was born to be a king, he felt like a man—like a king—who could afford to be tender because he was strong.

He scarcely slept that night, and even though he heard his little lark singing in the sunrise, he barely listened to it. Things more serious and important had take possession of his mind.

"Suppose," thought he, "I were to do as she says, and go out in the world, no matter how it hurts me—the world of people, active people, as active as that boy I saw. They might only laugh at me—poor helpless creature that I am. But still I might show them I could do something. At any rate, I might go and see if there were anything for me to do. Godmother, help me!"

It was so long since he had asked her help that he was hardly surprised when he got no answer— only the little lark outside the window sang louder and louder, and the sun rose, flooding the room with light.

Prince Dolor sprang out of bed, and began dressing himself, which was hard work, for he was not used to it—he had always been accustomed to depend upon his nurse for everything.

"But I must now learn to be independent," thought he. "Fancy a king being dressed like a baby!"

So he did the best he could—awkwardly but cheerily—and then he leaped to the corner where lay his traveling cloak, untied it as before, and watched it unrolling itself—which it did rapidly, with a hearty good will, as if quite tired of idleness. So was Prince Dolor—or felt as if he were. He jumped into the middle of it, said his charm, and was out through the skylight immediately.

"Good-by, pretty lark!" he shouted, as he passed it on the wing, still warbling its carol to the newly risen sun. "You have been my pleasure, my delight; now I must go and work. Sing to old nurse till I come back again. Perhaps she'll hear you—

perhaps she won't—but it will do her good all the same. Good-by!''

But, as the cloak hung irresolute in air, he suddenly remembered that he had not determined where to go—indeed, he did not know, and there was nobody to tell him.

"Godmother," he cried, in much perplexity, "you know what I want—at least, I hope you do, for I hardly do myself—take me where I ought to go. Show me whatever I ought to see—never mind what I like to see," as a sudden idea came into his mind that he might see many painful and disagreeable things. But this journey was not for pleasure—as before. He was not a baby now, to do nothing but play—big boys do not always play. Nor men neither—they work. This much Prince Dolor knew—though very little more.

As the cloak started off, traveling faster than he had ever known it do to—through sky-land and cloud-land, over freezing mountaintops, and desolate stretches of forest, and smiling cultivated plains, and great lakes that seemed to him almost as shoreless as the sea—he was often rather frightened. But he crouched down, silent and quiet; what was the use of making a fuss? And, wrapping himself up in his bearskin, he waited for what was to happen.

After some time he heard a murmur in the distance, increasing more and more till it grew like a hum of a gigantic hive of bees. And, stretching his chin over the rim of his cloak, Prince Dolor saw—far, far below him, yet, with his gold spectacles and silver ears on, he could distinctly hear and see—what?

Most of us have some time or other visited a great metropolis—have wandered through its network of streets—lost ourselves in its crowds of people—looked up at all its tall rows of houses, its grand public buildings, churches, and squares. Also, perhaps, we have peeped into its miserable little back alleys, where dirty children play in gutters all day and half the night—even young boys go about picking pockets, with nobody to tell them it is wrong except the policeman, and he simply takes them off to prison. And all this wretchedness is close behind the grandeur—like the two sides of the leaf of a book.

An awful sight is a large city, seen anyhow from anywhere. But, suppose you were to see it from the upper air, where, with your eyes and ears open, you could take in everything at once? What would it look like? How would you feel about it? I hardly know myself. Do you?

Prince Dolor had need to be a king—that is, a boy with a kingly nature—to be able to stand such a sight without being utterly overcome. But he was very much bewildered—as bewildered as a blind person who is suddenly made to see.

He gazed down on the city below him, and then put his hand over his eyes.

"I can't bear to look at it, it is so beautiful—so dreadful. And I don't understand it—not one bit. There is nobody to tell me about it. I wish I had somebody to speak to."

"Do you? Then pray speak to me. I was always considered good at conversation."

The voice that squeaked out this reply was an excellent imitation of the human one, though it came only from a bird. No lark this time, however, but a great black and white creature that flew into the cloak, and began walking round and round on the edge of it with a dignified stride, one foot before the other, like any unfeathered biped you could name.

"I haven't the honor of your acquaintance, sir," said the boy politely.

"Ma'am, if you please. I am a mother bird, and my name is Mag, and I shall be happy to tell you everything you want to know. For I know a great deal; and I enjoy talking. My family is of great antiquity. We have built in this palace for hundreds—that is to say, dozens of years. I am intimately acquainted with the King, the Queen, and the little Princes and Princesses—also the maids of honor, and all the inhabitants of the city. I talk a good deal, but I always talk sense, and I dare say I should be exceedingly useful to a poor little ignorant boy like you."

"I am a prince," said the other gently.

"All right. And I am a magpie. You will find me a most respectable bird."

"I have no doubt of it," was the polite answer —though he thought in his own mind that Mag must have a very good opinion of herself. But she was a lady and a stranger, so of course he was civil to her.

She settled herself at his elbow, and began to chatter away, pointing out with one skinny claw, while she balanced herself on the other, every object of interest, evidently believing, as no doubt all its inhabitants did, that there was no capital in the world like the great metropolis of Nomansland.

I have not seen it, and therefore cannot describe it, so we will just take it upon trust, and suppose it to be, like every other fine city, the finest city that ever was built. Mag said so—and of course she knew.

Nevertheless, there were a few things in it which surprised Prince Dolor—and, as he had said, he could not understand them at all. One half the people seemed so happy and busy—hurrying up and down the full streets, or driving lazily along the parks in their grand carriages, while the other half were so wretched and miserable.

"Can't the world be made a little more equal? I would try to do it if I were a king."

"But you're not the King: only a little goose of a boy," returned the magpie loftily. " And I'm here not to explain things, only to show them. Shall I show you the royal palace?"

It was a very magnificent palace. It had terraces and gardens, battlements and towers. It extended over acres of ground, and had in it rooms enough to accommodate half the city. Its windows looked in all directions, but none of them had any particular view—except a small one, high up toward the roof, which looked out on the Beautiful Mountains. But since the Queen died there it had been closed, boarded up, indeed, the magpie said. It was so little and inconvenient that nobody cared to live in it. Besides, the lower apartments, which had no view, were magnificent—worthy of being inhabited by the King.

"I should like to see the King," said Prince Dolor.

Chapter 8

What, I wonder, would be most people's idea of a king? What was Prince Dolor's?

Perhaps a very splendid personage, with a crown on his head and a scepter in his hand, sitting on a throne and judging the people. Always doing right, and never wrong—"The king can do no wrong" was a law laid down in olden times. Never cross, or tired, or sick, or suffering; perfectly handsome and well dressed, calm and good-tempered, ready to see and hear everybody, and discourteous to nobody; all things always going well with him, and nothing unpleasant ever happening.

This, probably, was what Prince Dolor expected to see. And what did he see? But I must tell you how he saw it.

"Ah," said the magpie, "no levee today. The King is ill, though his Majesty does not wish it to be generally known—it would be so very inconvenient. He can't see you, but perhaps you might like to go and take a look at him in a way I often do? It is so very amusing.''

Amusing, indeed!

The Prince was just now too much excited to talk much. Was he not going to see the King his uncle, who had succeeded his father and dethroned himself; had stepped into all the pleasant things that he, Prince Dolor, ought to have had, and shut him up in a desolate tower? What was he like, this great, bad, clever man? Had he got all the things he wanted, which another ought to have had? And did he enjoy them?

''Nobody knows,'' answered the magpie, just as if she had been sitting inside the Prince's heart, instead of on the top of his shoulder. ''He is a king, and that's enough. For the rest nobody knows.''

As she spoke, Mag flew down onto the palace roof, where the cloak had rested, settling down between the great stacks of chimneys as comfortably as if on the ground. She pecked at the tiles with her beak—truly she was a wonderful bird—and immediately a little hole opened, a sort of door, through which could be seen distinctly the chamber below.

''Now look in, my Prince. Make haste, for I must soon shut it up again.''

But the boy hesitated. ''Isn't it rude?— won't they think us intruding?''

''Oh, dear no! There's a hole like this in every palace; dozens of holes, indeed. Everybody know it, but nobody speaks of it. Intrusion! Why, though the royal family are supposed to live shut up behind stone walls ever so thick, all the world knows that they live in a glass house where everybody can see them and throw a stone at them. Now pop down on your knees, and take a peep at his Majesty!"

His Majesty!

The Prince gazed eagerly down into a large room, the largest room he had ever beheld, with furniture and hangings grander than anything he could have ever imagined. A stray sunbeam, coming through a crevice of the darkened windows, struck across the carpet, and it was the loveliest carpet ever woven—just like a bed of flowers to walk over; only nobody walked over it, the room being perfectly empty and silent.

"Where is the King?" asked the puzzled boy.

"There," said Mag, pointing with one wrinkled claw to a magnificent bed, large enough to contain six people. In the center of it, just visible under the silken counterpane—quite straight and still—with its head on the lace pillow, lay a small figure, something like wax-work, fast asleep—very fast asleep! There were a number of sparkling rings on the tiny yellow hands, that were curled a little, helplessly, like a baby's, outside the coverlet. The eyes were shut, the nose looked sharp and thin, and the long gray beard hid the mouth and lay over the breast. A sight not ugly nor frightening, only solemn and quiet. And so very silent—two little flies buzzing about the curtains of the bed being the only audible sound.

"Is that the King?" whispered Prince Dolor.

"Yes," replied the bird.

He had been angry—furiously angry—ever since he knew how his uncle had taken the crown, and sent him, a poor little helpless child, to be shut up for life, just as if he had been dead. Many times the boy had felt as if, king as he ws, he should like to strike him, this great, strong, wicked man.

Why, you might as well have struck a baby! How helpless he lay, with his eyes shut, and his idle hands folded. They had no more work to do, bad or good.

"What is the matter with him?" asked the Prince.

"He is dead," said the magpie, with a croak.

No, there was not the least use in being angry with him now. On the contrary, the Prince felt almost sorry for him, except that he looked so peaceful with all his cares at rest. And this is being dead? So even kings died?

"Well, well, he hadn't an easy life, folk say, for all his grandeur. Perhaps he is glad it is over. Good-by, your Majesty."

With another cheerful tap of her beak, Mistress Mag shut down the little door in the tiles, and Prince Dolor's first and last sight of his uncle was ended.

He sat in the center of his traveling cloak, silent and thoughtful.

"What shall we do now?" said the magpie. "There's nothing much more to be done with his Majesty, except a fine funeral, which I shall certainly go and see. All the world will. He interested the world exceedingly when he was alive, and he ought to do it now he's dead—just once more. And since he can't hear me, I may as well say that, on the whole, his Majesty is much better dead than alive—if we can only get somebody in his place. There'll be such a row in the city presently. Suppose we float up again and see it all—at a safe distance, though. It will be such fun!''

"What will be fun?"

"A revolution."

Whether anybody except a magpie would have called it "fun" I don't know, but it certainly was a remarkable scene.

As soon as the cathedral bell began to toll and the minute guns to fire, announcing to the kingdom that it was without a king, the people gathered in crowds, stopping at street corners to talk together. The murmur now and then rose into a shout, and the shout into a roar. When Prince Dolor, quietly floating in upper air, caught the sound of their different and opposite cries, it seemed to him as if the whole city had gone mad together.

"Long live the King!" "The King is dead—down with the King!" "Down with the crown, and the King too!" "Hurrah for the republic!" "Hurrah for no government at all!"

Such were the shouts which traveled up to the traveling cloak. And then began—oh, what a scene!

When you children are grown men and women—or before—you will hear and read in books about what are called revolutions—earnestly I trust that neither I nor you may ever see one. But they have happened, and may happen again, in other countries besides Nomansland, when wicked kings have helped to make their people wicked too, or out of an unrighteous nation have sprung rulers equally bad; or, without either of these causes, when a restless country has fancied any change better than no change at all.

For me, I don't like changes, unless I am pretty sure that they are for good. And how good can come out of absolute evil—the horrible evil that went on this night under Prince Dolor's very eyes—soldiers shooting down people by hundreds in the streets, scaffolds erected, and heads dropping off—houses burned, and women and children murdered—this is more than I can understand.

But all these things you will find in history, my children, and must by and by judge for yourselves the right and wrong of them, as far as anybody ever can judge.

Prince Dolor saw it all. Things happened so fast one after another that they quite confused his faculties.

"Oh, let me go home," he cried at last, stopping his ears and shutting his eyes; "only let me go home!" For even his lonely tower seemed home, and its dreariness and silence absolute paradise after all this.

"Good-by, then," said the magpie, flapping her wings. She had been chatting incessantly all day and all night, for it was actually thus long that Prince Dolor had been hovering over the city, neither eating nor sleeping, with all these terrible things happening under his very eyes.

"You've had enough, I suppose, of seeing the world?"

"Oh, I have—I have!" cried the Prince, with a shudder.

"That is, till next time. All right, your Royal Highness. You don't know me, but I know you. We may meet again sometime."

She looked at him with her clear, piercing eyes, sharp enough to see through everything, and it seemed as if they changed from bird's eyes to human eyes—the very ones of his godmother, whom he had not seen for ever so long. But the minute afterward she became only a bird, and with a screech and a chatter, spread her wings and flew away.

Prince Dolor fell into a kind of swoon of utter misery, bewilderment, and exhaustion, and when he awoke he found himself in his own room—alone and quiet—with the dawn just breaking, and the long rim of yellow light in the horizon glimmering through the windowpanes.

Chapter 9

When Prince Dolor sat up in bed, trying to remember where he was, whither he had been, and what he had seen the day before, he perceived that his room was empty.

Generally his nurse rather worried him by breaking his slumbers, coming in and ''setting things to rights,'' as she called it. Now the dust lay thick upon chairs and tables. There was no harsh voice heard to scold him for not getting up immediately, which, I am sorry to say, this boy did not always do. For he so enjoyed lying still, and thinking lazily about everything or nothing, that, if he had not tried hard to avoid, it he would certainly have become like those celebrated

Two little men
Who lay in their bed till the clock struck ten.

It was striking ten now, and still no nurse was to

be seen. He was rather relieved at first, for he felt so tired. And besides, when he stretched out his arm, he found to his dismay that he had gone to bed in his clothes.

Very uncomfortable he felt, of course; and just a little frightened. Especially when he began to call and call again, but nobody answered. Often he used to think how nice it would be to get rid of his nurse and live in this tower all by himself—like a sort of monarch, able to do everything he liked, and leave undone all that he did not want to do. But now that this seemed really to have happened, he did not like it at all.

"Nurse—dear nurse—please come back!" he called out. "Come back, and I will be the best boy in all the land."

And when she did not come back, and nothing but silence answered his lamentable call, he very nearly began to cry.

"This won't do," he said at last, dashing the tears from his eyes. "It's just like a baby, and I'm a big boy—shall be a man someday. What has happened? I wonder. I'll go and see."

He sprang out of bed—not to his feet, alas! but to his poor little weak knees, and crawled on them from room to room. All the four chambers were deserted—not forlorn or untidy, for everything seemed to have been done for his comfort—the breakfast and dinner things were laid, the food spread in order. He might live "like a prince," as the proverb is, for several days. But the place was entirely forsaken—there was evidently not a creature but himself in the solitary tower.

A great fear came over the poor boy. Lonely as his life had been, he had never known what it was to be absolutely alone. A kind of despair seized him—no violent anger or terror, but a sort of patient desolation.

"What in the world am I to do?" thought he, and sat down in the middle of the floor, half inclined to believe that it would be better to give up entirely, lay himself down, and die.

This feeling, however, did not last long, for he was young and strong, and, I said before, by nature a very courageous boy. There came into his head, somehow or other, a proverb that his nurse had taught him—the people of Nomansland were very fond of proverbs—

> For every evil under the sun
> There is a remedy, or there's none;
> If there is one, try to find it—
> If there isn't, never mind it.

"I wonder is there a remedy now, and could I find it?" cried the Prince, jumping up and looking out the window.

No help there. He saw only the broad, bleak, sunshiny plain—that is, at first. But by and by, in the circle of mud that surrounded the base of the tower, he perceived distinctly the marks of a horse's feet, and just in the spot where the deaf-mute was accustomed to tie up his great black charger, while he himself ascended, there lay the remains of a bundle of hay and a feed of corn.

"Yes, that's it. He has come and gone,

taking nurse away with him. Poor nurse! how glad she would be to go!''

That was Prince Dolor's first thought. His second—wasn't it natural?—was a passionate indignation at her cruelty—at the cruelty of all the world toward him, a poor little helpless boy. Then he determined, forsaken as he was, to try and hold on to the last, and not to die as long as he could possibly help it.

Anyhow, it would be easier to die here than out in the world, among the terrible doings which he had just beheld—from the midst of which, it suddenly struck him, the deaf-mute had come, contriving somehow to make the nurse understand that the King was dead, and she need have no fear in going back to the capital, where there was a grand revolution, and everything turned upside down. So, of course, she had gone.

"I hope she'll enjoy it, miserable woman—if they don't cut off her head, too.''

And then a kind of remorse smote him for feeling so bitterly toward her, after all the years she had taken care of him—grudgingly, perhaps, and coldly; still she had taken care of him, and that even to the last. For, as I have said, all his four rooms were as tidy as possible, and his meals laid out, that he might have no more trouble than could be helped.

"Possibly she did not mean to be cruel. I won't judge her,'' said he. And afterward he was very glad that he had so determined.

For the second time he tried to dress himself, and then to do everything he could for himself—

even to sweeping up the hearth and putting on more coals. "It's a funny thing for a prince to have to do," said he, laughing. "But my godmother once said princes need never mind doing anything."

And then he thought a little of his godmother. Not of summoning her, or asking her to help him—she had evidently left him to help himself, and he was determined to try his best to do it, being a very proud and independent boy—but he remembered her tenderly and regretfully, as if even she had been a little hard upon him— poor, forlorn boy that he was. But he seemed to have seen and learned so much within the last few days that he scarcely felt like a boy, but a man—until he went to bed at night.

When I was a child, I used often to think how nice it would be to live in a little house all by my own self—a house built high up in a tree, or far away in a forest, or halfway up a hillside—so deliciously alone and independent. Not a lesson to learn—but no! I always liked learning my lessons. Anyhow, to choose the lessons I liked best, to have as many books to read and dolls to play with as ever I wanted: above all, to be free and at rest, with nobody to tease or trouble or scold me, would be charming. For I was a lonely little thing, who liked quietness—as many children do; which other children, and sometimes grown-up people even, cannot understand. And so I can understand Prince Dolor.

After his first despair, he was not merely comfortable, but actually happy in his solitude, doing everything for himself, and enjoying everything by himself—until bedtime. Then he did not like it at all. No more, I suppose, than other children would have liked my imaginary house in a tree when they had had sufficient of their own company.

But the Prince had to bear it—and he did bear it, like a prince—for fully five days. All that time he got up in the morning and went to bed at night without having spoken to a creature, or, indeed, having heard a single sound. For even his little lark was silent. And as for his traveling cloak, either he never thought about it, or else it had been spirited away—for he made no use of it, nor attempted to do so.

A very strange existence it was, those five lonely days. He never entirely forgot it. It threw him back upon himself—in a way that all of us have to learn when we grow up, and are the better for it; but it is somewhat hard learning.

On the sixth day Prince Dolor had a strange composure in his look, but he was very grave and thin and white. He had nearly come to the end of his provisions—and what was to happen next? Get out of the tower he could not. The ladder the deaf-mute used was always carried away again; and if it had not been how could the poor boy have used it? And even if he slung or flung himself down, and by miraculous chance came alive to the foot of the tower, how could he run away?

Fate had been very hard on him, or so it seemed.

He made up his mind to die. Not that he wished to die. On the contrary, there was a great deal that he wished to live to do; but if he must die, he must. Dying did not seem so very dreadful; not even to lie quiet like his uncle, whom he had entirely forgiven now, and never be miserable or naughty any more, and escape all those horrible things that he had seen going on outside the palace, in that awful place which was called "the world."

"It's a great deal nicer here," said the poor little Prince, and collected all his pretty things round him: his favorite pictures, which he thought he should like to have near him when he died; his books and toys—no, he had ceased to care for toys now; he only liked them because he had done so as a child. And there he sat very calm and patient, like a king in his castle, waiting for the end.

"Still, I wish I had done something first—something worth doing, that somebody might remember me by," thought he. "Suppose I had grown a man, and had had work to do, and people to care for, and was so useful and busy that they liked me, and perhaps even forgot I was lame? Then it would have been nice to live, I think."

A tear came into the little fellow's eyes, and he listened intently through the dead silence for some hopeful sound.

Was there one?—was it his little lark, whom he had almost forgotten? No, nothing half so sweet. But it really was something—something which came nearer and nearer, so that there was no mistaking it. It was the sound of a trumpet, one of the great silver trumpets so admired in

Nomansland. Not pleasant music, but very bold, grand, and inspiring.

As he listened to it the boy seemed to recall many things which had slipped his memory for years, and to nerve himself for whatever might be going to happen.

What had happened was this.

The poor condemned woman had not been such a wicked woman after all. Perhaps her courage was not wholly disinterested, but she had done a very heroic thing. As soon as she heard of the death and burial of the King and of the changes that were taking place in the country, a daring idea came into her head—to set upon the throne of Nomansland its rightful heir. Thereupon she persuaded the deaf-mute to take her away with him, and they galloped like the wind from city to city, spreading everywhere the news that Prince Dolor's death and burial had been an invention concocted by his wicked uncle—that he was alive and well, and the noblest young Prince that ever was born.

It was a bold stroke, but it succeeded. The country, weary perhaps of the late King's harsh rule, and yet glad to save itself from the horrors of the last few days, and the still further horrors of no rule at all, and having no particular interest in the other young Princes, jumped at the idea of this Prince, who was the son of their late good King and the beloved Queen Dolorez.

"Hurrah for Prince Dolor! Let Prince Dolor be our sovereign!" rang from the end to end of the kingdom. Everybody tried to remember what a dear baby he once was—how like his mother, who had been so sweet and kind, and his father, the finest-looking king that ever reigned. Nobody remembered his lameness— or, if they did, they passed it over as a matter of no consequence. They were determined to have him reign over them, boy as he was—perhaps just because he was a boy, since in that case the great nobles thought they should be able to do as they liked with the country.

Accordingly, with a fickleness not confined to the people of Nomansland, no sooner was the late King laid in his grave than they pronounced him to have been a usurper; turned all his family out of the palace, and left it empty for the reception of the new sovereign, whom they went to fetch with great rejoicing, a select body of lords, gentlemen, and soldiers traveling night and day in solemn procession through the country until they reached Hopeless Tower.

There they found the Prince, sitting calmly on the floor—deadly pale, indeed, for he expected a quite different end from this, and was resolved, if he had to die, to die courageously, like a prince and a king.

But when they hailed him as Prince and King, and explained to him how matters stood, and went down on their knees before him, offering the crown (on a velvet cushion, with four golden tassels, each nearly as big as his head)— small though he was and lame, which lameness the courtiers pretended not to notice—there came such glow into his face, such a dignity into his demeanor, that he became beautiful, kinglike.

"Yes," he said, "if you desire it, I will be your king. And I will do my best to make my people happy."

Then there arose, from inside and outside the tower, such a shout as never yet was heard across the lonely plain.

Prince Dolor shrank a little from the deafening sound. "How shall I be able to rule all this great people? You forget, my lords, that I am only a little boy still."

"Not so very little," was the respectful answer. "We have searched in the records, and found that your Royal Highness—your Majesty, I mean—is fifteen years old."

"Am I?" said Prince Dolor; and his first thought was a thoroughly childish pleasure that he should now have a birthday, with a whole nation to keep it. Then he remembered that his childish days were done. He was a monarch now. Even his nurse, to whom, the moment he saw her, he had held out his hand, kissed it reverently, and called him ceremoniously "his Majesty the King."

"A king must be always a king, I suppose," said he half sadly, when, the ceremonies over, he had been left to himself for just ten minutes, to put off his boy's clothes and be reattired in magnificent robes, before he was conveyed away from his tower to the royal palace.

He could take nothing with him; indeed, he soon saw that, however politely they spoke, they would not allow him to take anything. If he was to be their king, he must give up his old life forever. So he looked with tender farewell on his old books, old toys, the furniture he knew so well, and the familiar plain in all its levelness—ugly yet pleasant, simply because it was familiar.

"It will be a new life in a new world," said he to himself; "but I'll remember the old things still. And, oh! if before I go I could but once see my dear old godmother."

While he spoke he had laid himself down on the bed for a minute or two, rather tired with his grandeur, and confused by the noise of the trumpets which kept playing incessantly down below. He gazed, half sadly, up to the skylight, whence there came pouring a stream of sun rays, with innumerable motes floating there, like a bridge thrown between heaven and earth. Sliding down it, as if she had been made of air, came the little old woman in gray.

So beautiful looked she—old as she was—that Prince Dolor was at first quite startled by the apparition. Then he held out his arms in eager delight.

"Oh, godmother, you have not forsaken me!"

"Not at all, my son. You may not have seen me, but I have seen you many a time."

"How?"

"Oh, never mind. I can turn into anything I please, you know. And I have been a bearskin rug, and a crystal goblet—and sometimes I have changed from inanimate to animate nature, put on feathers, and made myself very comfortable as a bird."

"Ha!" laughed the Prince, a new light breaking in upon him as he caught the infection of her tone, lively and mischievous. "Ha! ha! a lark, for instance?"

"Or a magpie," answered she, with a capital imitation of Mistress Mag's croaky voice. "Do you suppose I am always sentimental, and never funny? If anything makes you happy, gay, or grave, don't you think it is more than likely to come through your old godmother?"

"I believe that," said the boy tenderly, holding out his arms. They clasped one another in a close embrace.

Suddenly Prince Dolor looked very anxious. "You will not leave me now that I am a king? Otherwise I had rather not be a king at all. Promise never to forsake me!"

The little old woman laughed gaily. "Forsake you? that is impossible. But it is just possible you may forsake me. Not probable though. Your mother never did, and she was a queen. The sweetest queen in all the world was the Lady Dolorez."

"Tell me about her," said the boy eagerly. "As I get older I think I can understand more. Do tell me."

"Not now. You couldn't hear me for the trumpets and the shouting. But when you are come to the palace, ask for a long-closed upper room, which looks out upon the Beautiful Mountains. Open it and take it for your own. Whenever you go there you will always find me, and we will talk together about all sorts of things."

"And about my mother?"

The little old woman nodded—and kept

nodding and smiling to herself many times, as the boy repeated over and over again the sweet words he had never known or understood— "my mother—my mother."

"Now I must go," said she, as the trumpets blared louder and louder, and the shouts of the people showed that they would not endure any delay. "Good-by, good-by! Open the window and out I fly."

Prince Dolor repeated gaily the musical rhyme—but all the while tried to hold his god-mother fast.

Vain, vain! for the moment that a knocking was at his door the sun went behind a cloud, the bright stream of dancing motes vanished, and the little old woman with them—he knew not where.

So Prince Dolor quitted his tower—which he had entered so mournfully and ignominiously as a little helpless baby carried in the deaf-mute's arms —quitted it as the great King of Nomansland.

The only thing he took away with him was something so insignificant that none of the lords, gentlemen, and soldiers who escorted him with such triumphant splendor could possibly notice it—a tiny bundle, which he had found lying on the floor just where the bridge of sunbeams had rested. At once he had pounced upon it, and thrust it secretly into his bosom, where it dwindled into such small proportions that it might have been taken for a mere chest comforter, a bit of flannel, or an old pocket handkerchief.

It was his traveling cloak!

Chapter 10

Did Prince Dolor become a great king? Was he, though little more than a boy, "the father of his people," as all kings ought to be? Did his reign last long—long and happy? And what were the principal events of it, as chronicled in the history of Nomansland?

Why, if I were to answer all these questions I should have to write another book. And I'm tired, children; tired—as grown-up people sometimes are, though not always with play. (Besides, I have a small person belonging to me, who, though she likes extremely to listen to the word-of-mouth story of this book, grumbles much at the writing of it, and has run about the house clapping her hands with joy when mamma told her that it was nearly finished. But that is neither here nor there.)

I have related as well as I could the history of Prince Dolor, but with the history of Nomansland I am as yet unacquainted. If anybody knows it, perhaps he or she will kindly write it all down in another book. But mine is done.

However, of this I am sure, that Prince Dolor made an excellent king. Nobody ever does anything less well, not even the commonest duty of common daily life, for having such a godmother as the little old woman clothed in gray, whose name is—well, I leave you to guess. Nor, I think, is anybody less good, less capable of both work and enjoyment in afterlife, for having been a little unhappy in his youth, as the Prince had been.

I cannot take upon myself to say that he was always happy now—who is?—or that he had no cares; just show me the person who is quite free from them! But whenever people worried and bothered him—as they did sometimes, with state etiquette, state squabbles, and the like, setting up themselves and pulling down their neighbors—he would take refuge in that upper room which looked out on the Beautiful Mountains, and, laying his head on his godmother's shoulder, become calmed and at rest.

Also, she helped him out of any difficulty which now and then occurred—for there never was such a wise old woman. When the people of Nomansland raised the alarm—as sometimes they did—for what people can exist without a little fault-finding?—and began to cry out, "Unhappy is the nation whose king is a child," she would say to him gently, "You are a child. Accept the fact. Be humble—be teachable. Lean upon the wisdom of others till you have gained your own."

He did so. He learned how to take advice before attempting to give it, to obey before he could righteously command. He assembled round him all the good and wise of his kingdom—laid all its affairs before them, and was guided by their opinions until he had maturely formed his own.

This he did sooner than anybody would have imagined who did not know of his godmother and his traveling cloak—two secret blessings, which, though many guessed at, nobody quite understood. Nor did they understand why he loved so the little upper room, except that it had been his mother's room, in the window of which, as people remembered now, she had used to sit for hours watching the Beautiful Mountains.

Out that window he used to fly—not very often. As he grew older, the labors of state prevented the frequent use of his traveling cloak; still he did use it sometimes. Only now it was less for his own pleasure and amusement than to see something or investigate something for the good of the country. But he prized his godmother's gift as dearly as ever. It was a comfort to him in all his vexations, an enhancement of all his joys. It made him almost forget his lameness—which was never cured.

However, the cruel things which had been once foreboded of him did not happen. His misfortune was not such a heavy one, after all. It proved to be of much less inconvenience, even to himself, than had been feared. A council of eminent surgeons and mechanicians invented for him a wonderful pair of crutches, with the help of which, though he never walked easily or gracefully, he did manage to walk so as to be quite independent. And such was the love his people bore him that they never heard the sound of his crutches on the marble palace floors without a leap of the heart, for they knew that good was coming to them whenever he approached.

Thus, though he never walked in processions, never reviewed his troops mounted on a magnificent charger, nor did any of the things which make a show monarch so much appreciated, he was able to perform all the duties and to enjoy a great many of the pleasures of his rank. When he held his levees, not standing, but seated on a throne ingeniously contrived to hide his infirmity, the people thronged to greet him. When he drove out through the city streets, shouts followed him wherever he went—every countenance brightened as he passed, and his own, perhaps, was the brightest of all.

First, because, accepting his affliction as inevitable, he took it patiently; second, because, being a brave man, he bore it bravely, trying to forget himself, and live out of himself, and in and for other people. Therefore other people grew to love him so well that I think hundreds of his subjects might have been found who were almost ready to die for their poor lame king.

He never gave them a queen. When they implored him to choose one, he replied that his country was his bride, and he desired no other. But perhaps the real reason was that he shrank from any change; and that no wife in all the world would have been found so perfect, so lovable, so tender to him in all his weaknesses as his beautiful old godmother.

His twenty-four other godfathers and godmothers, or as many of them as were still alive, crowded around him as soon as he ascended the throne. He was very civil to them all, but adopted none of the names they had given him, keeping to the one by which he had been always known, though it had now almost lost its meaning; for King Dolor was one of the happiest and cheerful men alive.

He did a good many things, however, unlike most men and most kings, which a little astonished his subjects. First, he pardoned the condemned woman who had been his nurse, and ordained that from henceforth there should be no such thing as the punishment of death in Nomansland. All capital criminals were to be sent to perpetual imprisonment in Hopeless Tower and the plain round about it, where they could do no harm to anybody, and might in time do a little good, as the woman had done.

Another surprise he shortly afterward gave the nation. He recalled his uncle's family, who had fled away in terror to another country, and restored them to all their honors. By and by he chose the eldest son of his eldest cousin (who had been dead a year), and had him educated in the royal palace, as the heir to the throne. This little prince was a quiet, unobtrusive boy, so that everybody wondered at the King's choosing him when there were so many more. But as he grew into a fine young fellow, good and brave, they agreed that the King had judged more wisely than they.

"Not a lame prince, either," his Majesty observed one day, watching him affectionately. For he was the best runner, the highest leaper, the keenest and most active sportsman in the country. "One cannot make one's self, but one can sometimes help a little in the making of somebody else. It is well."

This was said, not to any of his great lords and ladies, but to a good old woman—his first homely nurse—whom he had sought for far and wide, and at last had found in her cottage among the Beautiful Mountains. He sent for her to visit him once a year, and treated her with great honor until she died. He was equally kind, though somewhat less tender, to his other nurse, who, after receiving her pardon, returned to her native town and grew into a great lady, and I hope a good one. But as she was so grand a personage now, any little faults she had did not show.

Thus King Dolor's reign passed year after year, long and prosperous. Whether he was happy—"as happy as a king"—is a question no human being can decide. But I think he was, because he had the power of making everybody about him happy, and did it too; also because he was his godmother's godson, and could shut himself up with her whenever he liked, in that quiet little room in view of the Beautiful Mountains, which nobody else ever saw or cared to see. They were too far off, and the city lay so low. But there they were, all the time. No change ever came to them; and I think, at any day throughout his long reign, the King would sooner have lost his crown than have lost sight of the Beautiful Mountains.

In course of time, when the little Prince his cousin was grown into a tall young man, capable of all the duties of a man, his Majesty did one of the most extraordinary acts ever known in a sovereign beloved by his people and prosperous in his reign. He announced that he wished to invest his heir with the royal purple—at any rate, for a time—while he himself went away on a distant journey, whither he had longed desired to go.

Everybody marveled, but nobody opposed him. Who could oppose the good King, who was not a young king now? And besides, the nation had a great admiration for the young Regent—and possibly a lurking pleasure in change.

So there was a fixed day when all the people whom it would hold assembled in the great square of the capital, to see the young Prince installed solemnly in his new duties, and undertaking his new vows. He was a very fine young fellow; tall and straight as a poplar tree, with a frank, handsome face—a great deal handsomer than the King's, some people said, but others thought differently. However, as his Majesty sat on his throne, with his gray hair falling from underneath his crown, and a few wrinkles showing in spite of his smile, there was something about his countenance which made his people, even while they shouted, regard him with a tenderness mixed with awe.

He lifted up his thin, slender hand, and there came a silence over the vast crowd immediately. Then he spoke, in his own accustomed way, using no grand words, but saying what he had to say in the simplest fashion, though with a clearness that struck their ears like the first song of a bird in the dusk of the morning.

"My people, I am tired; I want to rest. I have had a long reign, and done much work—at least, as much as I was able to do. Many might have done it better than I—but none with a better will. Now I leave it to others: I am tired, very tired. Let me go home."

There arose a murmur—of content or discontent none could well tell; then it died down again, and the assembly listened silently once more.

"I am not anxious about you, my people—my children," continued the King. "You are prosperous and at peace. I leave you in good hands. The Prince Regent will be a fitter king for you than I."

"No, no, no!" rose the universal shout—and those who had sometimes found fault with him shouted louder than anybody. But he seemed as if he heard them not.

"Yes, yes," said he, as soon as the tumult had a little subsided; and his voice sounded firm and clear. Some very old people, who boasted of having seen him as a child, declared that his face took a sudden change, and grew as young and sweet as that of the little Prince Dolor. "Yes, I must go. It is time for me to go. Remember me sometimes, my people, for I have loved you well. And I am going a long way, and I do not think I shall come back anymore."

He drew a little bundle out of his breast pocket —a bundle that nobody had ever seen before. It was small and shabby-looking, and tied up with many knots, which untied themselves in an instant. With a joyful countenance, he muttered over it a few half-intelligible words. Then, so suddenly that even those nearest to his Majesty could not tell how it came about, the King was away—away—floating right up in the air—upon something, they knew not what, except that it appeared to be as safe and pleasant as the wings of a bird.

And after him sprang a bird—a dear little lark, rising from whence no one could say, since larks do not usually build their nests on the pavement of city squares. But there it was, a real lark, singing far over their heads, louder and clearer and more joyful as it vanished farther into the blue sky.

Shading their eyes, and straining their ears, the astonished people stood until the whole vision disappeared like a speck in the clouds—the rosy clouds that overhung the Beautiful Mountains.

King Dolor was never again beheld or heard of in his own country. But the good he had done there lasted for years and years. He was long missed and deeply mourned—at least, so far as anybody could mourn one who was gone on such a happy journey.

Whither he went, or who went with him, it is impossible to say. But I myself believe that his godmother took him on his traveling cloak to the Beautiful Mountains. What he did there, or where he is now, who can tell? I cannot. But one thing I am quite sure of, that, wherever he is, he is perfectly happy.

And so, when I think of him, am I.

About the author:

Dinah Maria Mulock Craik

Dinah Maria Mulock Craik was an English novelist born in 1826. She is the author of numerous children's stories and poems.